Good To Go

MARG MCALISTER

BLUE GEM PUBLISHING

ALSO BY MARG McALISTER

SERIES 1

Good to Go

Georgie Be Good

Good Riddance

Up to No Good

In Good Hands

Too Good to be True

As Good as It Gets

Good Golly Miss Molly

Good Vibrations

A Rocking Good Christmas

SERIES 2

Good Intentions

A Good Result

No Good Reason

Good Fortune

CHAPTER 1
Breaking the News

Georgie turned away from the window, took a deep breath, and finally summoned up enough courage to say the unthinkable. She looked at her father, standing beside her vibrating with excitement, and prepared to spoil his day.

"Dad, there's something I need to talk with you about." She kept her voice low, but something about her tone made her brother Jerry turn his head to look at her.

She ignored him, waiting for her father to respond, and then realized he hadn't heard. Still staring out of the window of the third-floor executive office of Johnny B. Goode's RV Empire in Elkhart, Indiana—the empire *he* had built from the ground up—he was entranced by the sight of the biggest and swankiest motorhome ever to come off the factory floor.

It was huge. It was scarlet, with black decals. It had four slide-outs, and the interior was sure to have more leather than the Ritz.

It was completely over the top and in-your-face, and Johnny Goode loved it.

"Dad?"

"Imagine the reaction when I drive *that* baby into the Expo," he said with absolute joy. "With Jerry cruising in behind me."

"Except you must admit that black is so much classier than red," Jerry said, grinning at him. Crowding Georgie, he leaned forward to catch the first glimpse of a second motorhome, glinting ebony in the sun, winding its way along the broad avenues of the RV Empire.

"Not just *red*, Jerry," his stepmother Angela said reprovingly. "It's candy apple. My absolute favorite color." She watched her gleaming new motorhome glide majestically to a stop below them and sighed with pleasure. "Oh, Johnny, I adore it."

"And look—here comes yours, Georgie!" her husband said, slinging an arm around his daughter's shoulders. "Isn't it a beauty?"

Georgie followed his pointing finger to the third

motorhome, just rounding the corner from the factory, and sucked in a breath. Her father had been keeping it as a surprise for her, not even allowing her to see the blueprints.

It wasn't a giant lumbering palace, like her father's and Jerry's. Tradition dictated that she would arrive at the Expo in a smaller motorhome, the newest and most luxurious Class C, encouraging hundreds of women and retired couples to follow her lead and buy one for themselves. This one was sure to appeal, with champagne paint and a streamlined aerodynamic shape.

But it so wasn't *her*.

Her father finally seemed to realize that she wasn't displaying the same giddy delight the rest of them were. "Georgie, you're going to love it." He squeezed her shoulder. "Wait until you see inside. We hired that couple that won last year's Reno Rescue."

Georgie nodded, summoning up a smile. She was the head of interior design at the Goode RV Empire, but her father hadn't wanted her to do her own RV—all part of the surprise.

She hated the idea of letting him down, but every year, just before the Expo, it was the same thing. They all had to play a part in the traditional ad for the Johnny B. Goode RV Empire, with some excruciatingly bad play on the family name. *"For a really Goode deal, come to the family that has been in the RV business for thirty years! Here's a sneak peek at this year's Extra Goode Expo Deals!"*

Every year, the biggest and the best. She looked down at the scarlet monster again, and Jerry's black behemoth behind it, and the smaller one intended for her, just pulling up behind the first two.

Their chief engineer was now looking up at the window, beckoning them, a grin spread across his face. He beckoned and made a sweeping bow that encompassed all three motorhomes.

That was tradition too. A small film crew was already down there, getting footage of the three motorhomes as well as the Goode family up at the window, watching them arrive.

And, as usual, there was a growing crowd.

It was too *late.* She couldn't do this, not now. She should have said something earlier.

"Georgie?" Her father's normally good-humored face was creased in a frown. "What's wrong?"

"Dad, I—" She swallowed and looked back out of the window. Her gaze swept across a sea of motorhomes, an ocean of trailers and camper vans, and she focused on the one part of the Johnny B. Goode Empire that interested her.

The one she really, really loved.

The vintage trailer section.

Compared to the rest of the complex, vintage and retro was tiny. Growing, yes (everything Johnny B. Goode touched flourished) but minuscule, compared to the rest.

Georgie gathered up her courage and blurted, "It's lovely, Dad, but honestly, it's not *me*. I wanted to do something different this year."

"But what?" Then, following her gaze, he shook his head. "*Georgie*. No. Not vintage. Not for the Expo."

She lifted her chin. "But why not?"

"Why not? Why *not*?" Her brother joined in the conversation, looking at her in disbelief. "The Expo is the biggest show of the year. We're there to sell, and cutting edge is what it's all about."

"Exactly," she said. "That's my point. Vintage trailers are growing in popularity, especially ours: custom-made for those who want the vintage look with modern conveniences. They *are* cutting edge, Jerry. We've even got a waiting list for vintage gypsy models."

Jerry snorted. "Tricked-up little trailers. That's

not where the big money is. We should be dumping that division and making more room for the latest model RVs."

Georgie looked at him in horror. "Don't even think about it. And they're a lot more than 'tricked-up trailers'. They're modeled on gypsy caravans from Ireland and the UK and Romania. The Vardo caravan—"

"Georgie." Jerry pointed at the scene below. "Look down there. *Look,* and tell me what's attracting all the attention. It sure isn't little retro trailers."

Frowning, Georgie looked down again. The crowd was milling around the two biggest motorhomes, taking photos and impatiently waiting for someone to open the doors so they could see inside. Jerry's, huge and black and mean, with gold flashes along each side, seemed to be a big hit. Georgie knew there was black leather inside and some kind of fancy-pants new finish for the countertops.

Her father and Jerry had similar tastes, except Jerry liked his RVs to look tougher. It was a running joke in the yearly ads. Johnny B. Goode and his children Jerry B and Georgie B, cracking jokes and trying to outdo each other. Luxury on wheels. All three of them would turn up in a convoy to the Expo, to cameras flashing and TV cameras rolling.

Not this year. She had to take a stand sometime.

She took a deep breath and said firmly, "No. Sorry, but no. This year, I want to go vintage."

The other three turned from the huge expanse of glass overlooking the RV rooftops and the two gleaming new monsters below and stared at her.

Jerry frowned. Her father was baffled. Angela looked appalled.

"It's time we did something different," Georgie went on, the words spilling out. Instinctively, she reached for the phrases that would appeal to her father's media-hungry soul. "Can you imagine? Two big beautiful motorhomes with the last word in…uh…everything…and then, in I roll in a vintage gypsy trailer. Color. Contrast. A whole new demographic. The *publicity*."

She almost choked on that last word. She hated the whole media circus. But if it would get her what she wanted…

"And another thing," she said, her voice a little high. "I want to head up the vintage trailer division from now on. Turning up in one to the Expo would turbocharge sales."

"You?" Jerry's frown grew deeper. "But you're

our chief interior designer and stylist. You haven't got time to head up Vintage."

That made her see red. "Of course I do. You're our communications specialist, but you still head up Class A and truck campers. That's *three* things."

"Sales and design are not anywhere near aligned," Jerry said, as though explaining it to a three-year-old. "You hate sales. You're the creative type."

"I sold three vintage trailers last week."

"I sold thirteen motorhomes, two fifth wheels, three upmarket trailers, and two vintage trailers." Jerry grinned at her. "Dad and I sell RVs. *You* decorate. End of story."

Choking down a fervent desire to punch him on his smug nose, Georgie counted to three and looked at her father. "Dad?"

Johnny B. Goode said nothing for a moment, just staring at her as you would a mouse that turned on a lion. Then she saw it in his face. He agreed with her brother: the men should handle the sales. He just didn't know how to tell her because he did truly love his daughter.

And Vintage? He scarcely noticed it was there.

Georgie had had enough.

"In that case," she said, "this year's family ad is

going to have just two of you. Since you seem to be the brains behind the…" she cast a glance out at the hundreds of RVs, their rooftop solar panels glinting in the sun, "…the *Empire*, you can have it."

"Georgie." His joy in his brand new Extreme RV dulled, her father reached out a placating hand. "Don't do this."

Georgie barely heard him. "I'm going to take the Vardo that I just finished," she said, "and I'm going on the road. I'll meet you at the Expo."

"You can't just take it. Not like that," Jerry objected. "It's our best demo model."

"I'll buy it." Fury rising in her chest, she glared at him. "*And* the truck we customized to tow it."

"You can't afford it." Jerry was practically nose-to-nose with her, the expression on his handsome face half patronizing, half irritated.

Georgie laughed. "I don't spend every cent I earn like you do, Jerry. Ten years' worth of savings? I can afford it."

Her father finally spoke up. "Stop it, Jerry." He reached for her hand. "Georgie, I can see you're serious. You don't have to buy it, don't be silly. But let's strike a deal. If you want to head up vintage trailers—and tow the gypsy trailer to this year's Expo—then you have to prove yourself. Go ahead, take it on the road. But I'm going to set you a sales target for the next month. If you meet it, you win. OK?"

Hardly able to believe her ears, Georgie flew at him. "Oh, Dad! Yes! *Yes!*" She hugged him hard and felt the rumble of his laughter.

"You haven't heard the sales target yet."

"I don't care. I agree." She was dizzy. She was going to take the gypsy trailer on the road! She loved, loved, *loved* vintage. You could sell anything if you were passionate enough. Easy. Easy!

"And to make it interesting," Johnny B. Goode said smoothly, "I'm going to set you the same target, Jerry. May the best Goode win."

CHAPTER 2

Rosa's Gift

Georgie took one last look around the inside of her beautiful gypsy trailer, letting her eyes rest on each divine inch. The sumptuous bed with its rich quilt the color of plump raspberries, with accents of gold and midnight blue and forest green. The soft drapes that fell to enclose the bed. The carved beauty of the door to the compact bathroom.

Her gaze lifted to the glowing stained glass inserts just under the roof and then moved on to the warm timber cupboards and the efficient black cooker that looked like an antique but worked as well as the modern version installed in her father's latest motorhome.

Then something out of place caught her eye.

Was that a *crystal ball?*

It was.

It had to be a peace offering from her father. Her heart melted. He was a lovely man, despite his acquisitive soul. He knew how much this meant to her.

A crystal ball for her gypsy trailer. A smile curving her lips, she reached up to the intricately carved shelf above the small table and lifted down the gleaming sphere.

It… hummed.

That was the only way she could put it. Tentatively running a finger over it, she drew in a breath. The thing felt almost alive in her hands.

Where had he got it? It was exactly like the one—

"So. You found it," came a croaking, self-satisfied voice.

Georgie jumped and turned to the shadow blackening the door opening, instinctively clamping her hands more firmly around the fragile ball. "Rosa!"

"Be careful with that." Her great-grandmother hauled herself up the steps with some effort, her feet encased in soft black slippers that had stretchy sides to accommodate her bunions. "It's hundreds of years old." She looked around her, her beady black eyes not missing a thing. "Huh, this is a bit fancier than the trailer I traveled in. But fortunes are fortunes, wherever they're told."

"This is yours?" Georgie looked from the crystal ball to Rosa and back again. "You're *giving* it to me?" She could scarcely believe it. It wasn't just exactly like the one in her great-grandmother's house, it was *the* one. The very same one Rosa had used for years to…

No, she told herself.

"I'm not going on the road to tell fortunes, Rosa," she said firmly, carefully putting the crystal ball back on the shelf. "I'm doing it to sell vintage trailers."

Rosa cackled.

Georgie flinched. She was never going to convince her great-grandmother that she didn't want this.

From the time she was a little girl, Rosa had rattled on about Georgie being the latest one to bear the Sight. "Born with a caul, you were," she had said with satisfaction when Georgie was eight. "I knew it would come out through the generations. You're the one."

Now, Rosa pulled her brightly woven gypsy

shawl around her bony shoulders and nodded. "You can deny it all you like, but the time has come. I'm passing it on to you."

Georgie closed her eyes for a second. Truth be told, Rosa looked as though she belonged in this trailer. She could sit there with her crystal ball and tell fortunes, with her old wrinkled mouth working and that direct clear cold black stare, and nervous clients would drink in every word.

But she's good at it, a small voice in the back of her mind said.

Georgie ignored it. "I'm not telling fortunes," she repeated.

"You don't have any say in it."

"Of course I do!"

"We'll see." Unruffled, Rosa smiled and Georgie hastily averted her gaze. Rosa was missing several teeth and nothing that her grandson Johnny B. Goode said would make her go anywhere near a dentist. Pink gums, eroded teeth, sunken lips... Georgie had lost track of how old Rosa was. In her nineties, for sure. She looked like she was well past a century, but moved like someone much younger.

Scary.

"I've seen it," Rosa said, reaching past Georgie to give the crystal ball an affectionate pat. "I saw this trailer, I saw the road. You've got people waiting for you."

"I've got *customers* waiting for me. Customers who want to buy a vintage trailer. Didn't Dad tell you? I have a sales target to meet. I'm going to be busy. Too busy for gazing into a crystal ball." Georgie pointed to a plastic tub on the floor. "See that? Full of sales brochures."

"See that?" Rosa pointed to the crystal ball. "Full of fortunes."

"I've never told fortunes in my life. I don't know how," Georgie said, gritting her teeth. "I'm not going to start, either."

"Yes, you have."

"I have *not*."

"The South Bend Fair."

Georgie frowned. The South Bend Fair?

"You were fifteen."

Fifteen. And suddenly, Georgie was back there, with her school friends Taylor and Josie. They had gone into the gypsy fortune-teller's tent, and the raven-haired woman there had invited them to try looking into the crystal ball themselves and telling her what they saw. "You can't count that! It was raining that day anyway." She waved a hand dismissively. "No wonder I thought of storms."

"You saw what was coming."

Georgie heaved a sigh. On that day, she had simply said the first thing that came into her head, something about a storm and accidents. Two days later, it had actually happened—but it had been easy to dismiss it as coincidence; there had been intermittent rain for days. She had promptly relegated it to the back of her mind.

Quite possibly because she knew that Great-Grandma Rosa could see into the future, and she had been a little bit afraid of Rosa all her life.

Still was.

And how did Rosa know about it, anyway? She hadn't been there.

"A coincidence," she said stubbornly. "Anyway, thanks for the crystal ball. It will add to the atmosphere. I'm sure it'll help to sell more trailers. Grandma Rosa... I really have to be heading off."

Her discomfort seemed to amuse her great-grandmother. "I suppose you do." She fixed her direct black gaze on Georgie. "You don't need to fear it, child. It will all come naturally."

Georgie shook her head. "I'm going to be heading up the vintage trailer division. To do that, I need to beat Jerry's sales figures." She hesitated. "I don't suppose you saw the results of *that* in your crystal ball?"

"I don't pass on everything I see." Rosa turned for the door, waving away the arm that Georgie instinctively offered to help her down the steps. "Time for me to go. Oh, and say hello to your Leo," she tossed back over her shoulder.

"To who?"

Rosa, disappearing down the steps, simply cackled again, and waved a dismissive hand.

"Who's Leo?" Georgie called after her.

Ignoring her, Rosa steamed off across the concrete apron to the front door of the office block, passing her grandson on the way. Johnny stopped for a moment to say something to her and then continued to where Georgie stood in the door of the trailer, frowning after her great-grandmother.

"Has Rosa been upsetting you again?" he asked, then without waiting for an answer, smoothed a hand over the carved handrail. "Beautiful work on this trailer. It will sell itself." He beamed at his daughter. "All ready to roll?"

"Twenty-five vintage trailers," Georgie said to him. "You set it at *twenty-five*."

"You said you didn't care what the quota was," he reminded her.

"But I thought you'd be fair. That's ridiculous. The most I've sold in a month was thirteen, and that was after a big RV show."

"Jerry says *he* can do it."

"You're playing us off against each other."

"Yep," he admitted cheerfully, giving her his trademark wide smile. His eyes were crafty. Her father was a born grifter. "Nothing comes too easily at Johnny B. Goode's RV Empire. When did I not make you work for your money?"

Never, she had to admit.

"Come here." He opened his arms wide, and she walked down three steps and into his hug. "I love you, girl. You'll do me proud."

"I will." Pushing aside the doubt, she kissed him on the cheek. "I'll be towing this Vardo trailer into the Expo, and I'll have the sales. It will be me heading up vintage trailers, not Jerry."

"He wants it. He wants it all."

"I know," she said, irritated. "And you'd let him have it."

"If he earned it. And you'll get it if *you* earn it." He gave her a little shake. "Come on, girl, have some confidence in yourself."

"I do. I really do." She looked over his shoulder

to where Rosa was disappearing through the front door. "Was it your idea to bring Rosa here today?"

"She asked me to." He cocked a head sideways. "She told you about the crystal ball?" '

"Yes. I saw it inside."

"She put it there this morning. Convinced that it's your destiny to follow in her footsteps. You picking this trailer was a sign, she said." He gave her a long look, uncharacteristically solemn. "You always could read people, Georgie. That's why you're so good with our customers. Don't dismiss it completely."

Georgie shook her head. She came from one stubborn family. Jerry wanted to head sales—in everything, including *her* vintage trailers. Her great-grandma, scary old bird, wanted her to become some gypsy fortune-teller. As if. She looked down at her t-shirt and jeans and compared herself to Rosa in her brightly patterned, embroidered outfits. No way. And now her *father* was telling her to think about it.

Sheesh.

She was twenty-nine, had three years of college plus years of experience behind her to show that she knew—*really* knew—design. Every RV she had outfitted proved it. Telling fortunes just didn't enter the picture.

She knew vintage trailers, too, and she could damn well sell them.

Now all she had to do was reach those targets.

"Goodbye, Dad." She hugged him again, with a thrilling feeling that she was just starting the next phase of her life. A whole division of the company, all hers.

Suck that up, brother Jerry.

She swung into the big powerful truck that had a custom wooden canopy painted to match her beautiful gypsy trailer and gunned the engine.

Georgie B. Goode was good to go.

CHAPTER 3

Are You Open for Business?

"Excuse me."

Georgie pegged her t-shirt to the tiny clothesline set up behind her trailer, and turned to see who was speaking. A woman in a loose plaid shirt and denim shorts was standing there, her gaze flicking between Georgie and the Vardo trailer. She spared a glance for the stained glass inserts, and then looked back at Georgie again.

Another potential sale, thought Georgie with satisfaction. People loved this trailer. They looked at their boring standard RVs and trailers, and they looked at her gypsy trailer, and they wanted one for themselves. As she had predicted, it was selling itself. Only three days on the road, stopping at a park just outside Fort Wayne the first day and now the big popular new RV park near Dayton for the last two days, and already she had converted two enquiries into deposits, with another woman interested. She was on track for those twenty-five sales.

"Good morning." She nodded and waited for the usual round of questions. How much did it cost, how long would it take to build, what was it like to tow…

"I know it's early, but I was just wondering… when are you open for business?"

"Well, now, I guess," Georgie said. "I'm open all the time, really."

"You are?" Heartened, the other woman smiled back. "How much do you charge?"

"There's no fee for a consultation."

"Wow," said the woman. "The last fortune teller I went to charged, like, twenty dollars before I even got through the door. Through the tent flap, that is. And that was for fifteen minutes."

"Fortune-teller?" Georgie's hopes dimmed. "No, sorry, I don't do that. I just consult with people who want to buy a trailer." Georgie glanced down at her usual t-shirt teamed with khaki shorts. Nope, nothing there to say 'fortune-teller'.

"Oh." Her face falling, the woman cast a glance at the Vardo. "It's very nice, but I don't want to buy one. I just want to know if this guy I'm going out with is the right one. For me. For, like, a life partner." She moved a step closer and gnawed at a fingernail. "He wants me to sell my motorhome and move in with him."

Don't do it, Georgie thought instinctively. She shrugged, trying to look blank.

The woman looked at her hopefully. "You are a real gypsy, right? You can do, like, readings?" She nodded at the trailer. "Tracey said that when you showed her through the trailer yesterday you had a crystal ball. She said you told her that it had been in your family for generations."

Damn. Georgie remembered Tracey. She had gossiped cheerfully for a solid hour, wanting to know everything about the Vardo trailer and gypsies and the retro scene and Georgie herself. Naturally she had spotted the crystal ball and asked about that too.

She shrugged. "It belonged to my great-grandmother. She's the fortune-teller, not me."

"Can I see it?"

No, Georgie wanted to say. *Go away.* But her natural good manners wouldn't let her. "Well…I guess."

She went inside to get it, intending to stand at

the top of the steps and hold it up for a moment, like the trophy at the Superbowl, before returning it to the shelf. But the woman was hot on her heels, and when Georgie turned around, she was standing right there at the entrance to the trailer.

"Wow," she said, staring around at everything. "This is, like, something out of a book! No wonder Tracey is dead set on buying one."

"She is?" said Georgie, diverted. "She didn't tell me that."

"She's going to work on Jamie. That's her husband. He wants to buy a new 4WD, so she's going to tell him he can have one if she can have one of these." She grinned, showing slightly crossed front teeth. "Tracey knows how to get what she wants. I'll give her two days, max, before she contacts you to order one. Or even today."

Georgie beamed at her. "That's great!"

In her hands, the crystal ball grew warm. Georgie felt an odd shiver creeping along her spine as she stared down at it. In the crystalline depths, something like smoke curled lazily.

Eeek.

"Are you sure you can't see anything in there? Did your great-grandma maybe teach you just a little bit?"

Georgie glanced up to see Kaylene staring at her hopefully.

Kaylene? Where did that come from? The woman hadn't introduced herself.

"I'm Georgie," she said, holding out her hand. "And your name?"

"Kaylene," the woman said.

Oh hell.

"Can you have a look? Just to see? I'm happy to pay," Kaylene said earnestly. "I really need to know."

Georgie wavered. The creepy feeling persisted, and the crystal ball grew warmer still.

"All right," she said. "But I don't really do this, you know. I can't guarantee that I'm right. So I can't charge you anything." She gestured at the L-shaped bench seat, upholstered in luxurious maroon velvet, tucked in behind her neat little wooden table. It was currently littered with Johnny B. Goode's RV Empire brochures and the two order forms that she had scanned and sent through to the office.

Georgie transferred the paperwork to the kitchen bench and sat down with Kaylene. They both stared at the crystal ball.

"Now what?" asked Kaylene. "Am I supposed to see something in there?"

How would I know? Georgie thought desperately. "Well, *can* you see anything?" she asked, covertly watching the swirly smoky stuff in the center of Rosa's crystal ball. She moved her hands back away a little. It was actually making her feel warm.

"No," Kaylene said. "It just looks like a ball. Is it really crystal or is it glass?"

"It's really crystal," Georgie assured her. Rosa wouldn't use anything but crystal, would she?

"So what do I do now?"

Georgie felt a drop of sweat on her forehead. This was like sitting for an exam when you not only hadn't studied, but the test paper was written in Martian. "Um. Just think about what you want to know," she suggested, and waited, mentally crossing her fingers.

Brian, came the name. Along with a creepy feeling in her spine.

She felt a sense of relief. At least she wasn't blank. "This, um, guy you're asking about. Is his name Brian?"

Kaylene looked disappointed. "No."

Brian, came the name again. It was almost clear

enough to make Georgie look over her shoulder to make sure they were alone.

"I keep getting Brian," she told Kaylene. "Would his middle name be Brian? Or his surname—like, O'Brien?" Oh God, she thought, I sound like one of those fake mediums who keep asking questions of some audience volunteer. *("I'm getting a male. Someone who recently passed. Would it be your father? No? Your uncle? No? There's definitely someone here who wants to talk to you…")*

"No," Kaylene said. "Definitely not Brian or O'Brien." Then her face cleared. "You're not talking about Brian Payne are you? The one in the big converted bus? He asked me out a couple of times before I started going out with Darryl." Her hand flew to her mouth. "Oops. Was I supposed to tell you his name?"

"I don't think it matters," Georgie said. "So, it's Darryl you're asking about?"

"Yes."

Brian, said the voice in her head insistently.

"Tell me about Brian Payne," she said.

Kaylene frowned. "He just travels around the country, working here and there. I don't know much about him."

"But you went out with him?"

"Yes. But he's not the one I want to know about. It's Darryl. He's talking about both of us living in his motorhome, getting married. Should I?" Her eyes moved from Georgie to the crystal ball, as though waiting for the answer to emerge.

Seriously out of her depth, Georgie said, "Why do you feel you need to consult a fortune-teller, Kaylene? Are you worried for some reason?"

"No. He's, like, good to me and all. Really good. But he keeps himself to himself. I don't know. My mother says I'm gullible." There was a note of defensiveness in the other woman's voice. "I don't have much luck with men."

Georgie looked back into the crystal ball and jumped in surprise. The swirly mist in there had parted to reveal something else. There were several shadowy women in there, just for an instant before they flickered out of sight. And again she felt the name, *Brian*…

She glanced up to find Kaylene watching her narrowly. "You know something, don't you? I saw your face. What is it?"

Georgie shook her head. "I'm not getting anything about Darryl. Just that you should be wary about someone called Brian." She could see the disappointment on Kaylene's face. "I'm sorry. I told you, I'm new to this."

"That's all right. I just wanted to be sure. I seem to pick 'em every time, the losers. Liars and cheats. I was hoping this time would be different."

"It might be." Georgie cast around for something to say. "But if you feel that something's not right, you should pay attention to that feeling."

"Yeah." Kaylene didn't move. "But how do I know when I've found a good one? I don't know what to do."

Since Georgie had been a gypsy fortune-teller for exactly ten minutes, and appeared to have failed miserably so far, she didn't have the answer to that one. She settled for: "If you're not sure, you shouldn't make any major decisions yet."

Kaylene sighed, shrugged and stood up. "Thanks for trying."

Georgie stood too. "Good luck, Kaylene."

"Thanks."

Georgie saw her to the door, and stood at the top of the steps watching her walk away, depression evident in every step.

Darn it. Georgie really, really wanted to help her, but she was hopeless at this.

Who was Brian? *Was* there a Brian?

The sound of laughter drifted across the park, and she glanced over to where a small crowd of people were gathered around a big shiny silver and black motorhome, parked on a site that had been vacant the night before. They were animated, looking at someone barely visible behind all the heads.

Georgie squinted at it, and then, as a woman moved and she caught sight of the logo on the motorhome, realization dawned. A dark wave of fury lanced through her.

Jerry.

Here, in her park, on *her* territory, in one of the big sales RVs with Johnny B. Goode's RV Empire emblazoned all over it. What was he *doing*?

CHAPTER 4

The Law According to Jerry

Georgie ran down the steps and pushed her way through the crowd.

"Hey, look who it isn't! My little sister Georgie." Jerry beamed at her, satisfaction all over his handsome face. He had his arm around Tracey's shoulder…and he was clutching an order form. "I've just been telling Tracey here that I could expedite her order so she could have her new gypsy trailer inside six weeks—as long as she signs today." He bestowed a smile that was all white teeth and dimples on Tracey, who looked both dazed and thrilled. "So she did!"

Georgie stared at Tracey.

Tracey, whom she had spent a whole hour with

the day before. Showing her every inch of her darling Vardo trailer.

Tracey's smile dimmed somewhat. "That's all right, isn't it? Jerry told me that it's a family company, so it didn't matter which one of you it was."

"That's perfectly fine," said Georgie with a fixed smile. "Jerry, when you've finished here, can you pop in and see me for a moment? There's something we need to discuss." She forced a casual wave to the group. "Excuse me. I need to finish my washing."

She wheeled around and strode back to the trailer.

What she *needed* was Jerry's head on a platter. They had it right in Game of Thrones: *off with his head!* Then stick it on a pike. She imagined Jerry's head grinning down from a pike right in front of Johnny B. Goode's RV Empire.

If she didn't suck at it, she might have consulted her crystal ball to see what the outcome of all this might be.

Furious, she stomped up the steps of her beautiful Vardo and threw herself down on the bed, staring up at the colors thrown by the sun coming through the glass inserts.

Suppose she hit Jerry over his pretty-boy head with the baseball bat she kept tucked down beside the bed, and he ended up in the ER, would she be arrested?

Probably. But it might be worth it.

Jerry took his time, and it was twenty minutes before he showed up and squeezed himself into the bench seat inside her trailer.

Georgie, sitting there with a cup of cold coffee in front of her, folded her arms and glared at him. "You can't do this. You're breaking the rules."

He wriggled and pushed at the table, which didn't give an inch. "There are no rules. Honestly, Georgie, how can you live in a space this big? Can't we go and talk in mine?"

"See, you don't even *like* vintage trailers." Crossly, she flicked the catch under the table and swung it out to make more space. "That's all you have to do. Dad designed it so everything adjusts. But you don't *know* that, because you don't know anything about them. Do you?"

"I know enough. Enough to nail the deal, which you didn't do. You would have let her escape."

"You cheated." Georgie stabbed a finger at him. "You let me show the trailer and then you stole my customer."

"No, Georgie, I was strategizing. If you knew anything about sales you'd know that. I knew you'd attract attention in your little gypsy trailer, and if I followed you I could close on all the ones you let through the net." He folded his arms and smiled, his warm brown eyes sympathetic, oozing sincerity. "You don't want to do this. Stop fighting it, Georgie girl. You enjoy styling and design. Let me do the selling."

Bereft of words, Georgie stared at him. Jerry had not only raided the family DNA bank for looks but had more than his fair share of intelligence and charm. Customers loved him. Men wanted to be his pal. Women wanted to bed him. Kids swarmed all over him. Even dogs liked him. It just wasn't fair. Jerry would mercilessly run over anyone in his path, and then they would thank him with their dying breath. How could she fight him?

I love vintage, she reminded herself. That's MY division.

"No," she said.

Jerry sighed. He gave her the kind of look a caring father would give a four-year-old who was acting out right before they did something stupid. The kind of look that said *I'll have to let you learn from experience.* She'd seen that look many times, from their father.

The difference was, her father cared about her.

But he cared about his RV Empire too. He meant what he said. If Jerry sold more vintage trailers, he was the one who'd get the job.

Well, she wasn't giving up that easily. If she had to be as devious as Jerry B. Goode, she damn well would.

Jerry was watching her while appearing not to. He drummed his fingers on the table and gazed around the trailer. Then he idly reached over and lifted the tea towel to see what was underneath.

A slow smile grew on his face when he saw the crystal ball.

"I do declare. You've been telling fortunes."

"I have not." Well, it wasn't quite a lie. She'd only told one fortune, and it was by accident.

"You never could lie, Georgie," he said, his fingers lightly tracing over the crystal. "This is Rosa's, isn't it? I recognize the base." His fingernail flicked the curling golden leaves decorating the stand. "She's been teaching you."

"No, she hasn't. I told her it's not for me."

Georgie slid out of the seat and removed it from his reach, tucking it back up on the shelf. "I was showing it to a customer. They all notice it because it adds… ambiance."

"Ambiance." He grinned at her. "You had a cloth over the top. Rosa always used to do that when she finished a reading. But she used black velvet, not a tea towel."

Still standing, she put her hands on her hips and went back to the matter at hand. "You're not going to follow me around everywhere, are you? Surely you're not that low."

"No," he said. "Well, I am that low, but I won't. I've got truck campers and fifth wheels and motorhomes to sell, too. Because that's what I *do*." He finally edged out of the seat and stood, his head almost touching the ceiling. "There are a couple of guys interested in our newest truck camper. I'm off to see them, now. And then I'm going to the vintage rally just outside of Columbus."

Rub it in, she thought sourly. Mr. Super Salesman. And dammit, she was heading for the Columbus rally, too. Was she going to run into Jerry everywhere?

"Maybe you *should* tell fortunes," he said. "That would give you a point of difference, wouldn't it?"

He laughed. "You could tell them that you see a retro trailer in their future. A carefree life on the road, in a charming vintage trailer. How could they resist? There you go, a free tip from The Master."

Annoyingly, he planted a kiss on her forehead on the way out. "Now I'm going to chat to my fans. Er, customers." He laughed.

Head on a pike, she thought viciously.

Going to the door, she watched him walk off into the distance until he was hailed by a trio of eager males—with females, as always, fluttering about in the background.

Don't waste your time, ladies, she thought. Jerry B. Goode loves himself too much to let anyone else into his heart.

She shot one last look at the gleaming Johnny B. Goode RV Empire sales unit, Jerry's home on the road until the Expo, and sighed.

Then, just as she was about to close the door and sulk for a while, she had an evil thought, and a slow smile formed.

Maybe she could…

No, she thought. *I couldn't.*

She stared at the sleek silver motorhome for a long moment, and then back to where Jerry was turning on the charm in the distance.

"There are no rules." The law according to Jerry.

"OK," she said to herself. "OK."

It took five minutes to wander casually over to his motorhome, glance over the two orders for vintage trailers that Jerry had carelessly tossed onto the table, put back the one that already bore his signature, and purloin the other.

Back in her trailer, she signed Tracey's order, scanned it, and sent it through to Johnny B. Goode's RV Empire in Indianapolis.

Take that, Jerry.

Three sales in three days.

Enormously cheered, she got down the crystal ball and gazed at it thoughtfully. It sat there innocently: bright and clear and cold, without offering so much as a whisper in her ear.

Maybe it *would* give her a point of difference.

Why not take lessons from Super Con himself?

Yes.

Tomorrow, she would go shopping for some clothes befitting most people's view of a gypsy fortune-teller.

CHAPTER 5

Found Out

G eorgie was having fun.

Dressing in vintage clothing was proving to be as much fun as styling a vintage trailer. A quick computer check told her where to find the kind of clothes she wanted, and within two hours she was back at the RV park, hauling shopping bags out of the back seat. She'd found a bright shawl with intricate embroidery—expensive, but it would give her the right look in mere seconds when draped over whatever she had on—several long skirts in rich dark colors, a couple of headscarves in varying patterns, and several tops. And a pair of Boho pants for comfort.

Fun, fun, fun.

She slammed the door and turned, and there was Jerry, sitting on the steps of her van. He pursed his lips at her.

Uh oh.

"So," Georgie said brightly. "Did you sell a truck camper or three?"

"Two signed on the dotted line. The third was a tire-kicker."

He didn't *look* mad. Maybe he hadn't realized yet. Maybe he would do all the paperwork tonight. Maybe he would put it off for a couple of days and she would be out of here before he knew.

His next words dashed that hope. "Nice move, Georgie," he said. "But you can give it back now."

She sent him a nervous smile. "Too late. I've signed it and sent it in. Can you move so I can get in?"

Instead, he leaned back, resting his elbows on the top step. His head cocked to one side, he studied her as though she were a beetle on a pin.

Georgie sighed, dropped her bags, and went around the back of the trailer to collect her camp chair from where she had been enjoying breakfast earlier in the morning sun. When she came back, he was examining her shopping.

"Hey!" she said. "That's private."

Undeterred, Jerry drew out the shawl and shook it out. He held it up and raised an eyebrow. "Just like Rosa's. You *are* going to do the gypsy thing."

Dammit, was Jerry going to know her every move? "I just thought I'd dress the part," she said, plunking herself down in the chair. "I don't know if I can fudge the telling fortunes bit."

He flicked the shawl outward and let it go so that it settled in a colorful drift over her knees. "Rosa thinks you can do it. She's been saying it for years. Have you tried?"

"I'm not Rosa," she said, thinking of her failed attempt to help Kaylene that morning. But what she could or couldn't do was none of Jerry's business.

He gave her a piercing look. "You do understand that snitching my sale has made me more determined than ever to beat you, don't you? By a big, big margin."

"I would expect nothing else."

"The gloves are off now, Georgie."

"You're the one who said 'there are no rules'."

Jerry laughed. "Who are you?" he asked. "And what have you done with the real Georgie?"

"You've never stolen my customers before."

"We've never been in direct competition before." Jerry smiled at her. "You going to offer me a cup of coffee?"

"No," she said. "I'm mad at you. I don't like the way you play the game. Go away, Jerry."

"OK." Jerry stayed where he was for a whole extra minute, watching her with a small smile and a gleam of anticipation in his eye. Silence was another tactic of Jerry's that Georgie knew well; he used it to advantage in sales situations. She wasn't going to bite.

"Well, I guess I'll see you around." Jerry stood and stretched. "One of the local distributors is picking me up for lunch. I'll be locking the motorhome while I'm gone."

"You should always do that anyway," said Georgie sweetly. "There are always thieves around. And con men."

"'Bye, Sis." He tugged at her hair on the way past. "Be seeing you."

Georgie thrust down a childish desire to retort, "Not if I see you first," and gathered her bags.

Forget Jerry, she told herself. *Just focus on selling. Whatever it takes.*

She went inside to turn herself into a gypsy.

Georgie couldn't see much in the small bathroom mirror, even when she angled her makeup mirror to glimpse another angle, but the part she could see looked authentic. She'd opted for a white peasant blouse with rich, intricate embroidery in a kaleidoscope of colors, including the deep green of her skirt.

Should she wear a scarf?

She tried it and assessed the effect; tied at the back like a kerchief, or just draped over her hair. Maybe not. Not right away. Just the blouse and skirt to begin with. No need to go overboard.

She contented herself with letting her hair flow loose over her shoulders, instead of tying it back.

The skirt swished around her when she walked: a feeling that would take some getting used to. Unless she was in corporate mode back at the dealership, she usually wore jeans or shorts.

The crystal ball caught her eye, and she stopped. Then she peered at the shelf beside it and saw a folded square of black velvet.

Her great-grandma had even given her the cloth she used to cover the crystal ball.

Georgie picked it up and, on impulse, rubbed it

against her cheek. "Better help me, Rosa," she whispered. "I have no idea what I'm doing..."

She held her breath for a moment, waiting for a sign. The velvet was warm against her cheek, but no messages floated her way.

No mysterious insights.

Oh well. She unfolded the cloth—which she could now see was worn in places from age—and tucked it around the crystal ball. Why it should be covered, she had no clue, but Rosa had always done it. "Fake it till you make it," she said under her breath. She really should look up 'how to read a crystal ball' on the Internet and find out if there were any shortcuts.

Fortune-Telling for Dummies?

Rosa, she remembered, read tea leaves and palms, too. And cards. She didn't use Tarot: just ordinary playing cards. Georgie—when she was too little to know she shouldn't encourage her great-grandmother—had once asked her why she did all of those things. Rosa had just cackled (she really did cackle, like the crack of a whip) and said that all the Sight came from the same place, and it didn't matter what you used.

Like that was helpful.

Anyway, back to the real world. By now, her washing should be dry.

Georgie swished her way to the door, feeling like a kid playing dress-up, and then promptly ruined the impression by tripping over the hem of her new skirt halfway down the steps. She barely had time to register that she was plunging headlong towards the ground before strong hands seized her and swung her out and around and safely onto her feet. "Whoa! That was a close one," said a voice with a British accent.

Georgie blinked and waited a second for her heart rate to slow before looking at her rescuer. There were two of him. She was seeing double.

No, there were two *gardeners*, both wearing t-shirts with the RV park logo. The bigger one let her go and grinned at her. "Lucky for you we came to fix your faucet."

"You did?" She glanced at where he was pointing and saw a mini-lake under her water fixture. Hastily, she hiked up her new skirt before it got soaked. "Is that my fault?"

"Don't think so." Her rescuer cast a look at the faucet. "Your fittings look new."

"They are. We just finished this trailer last week." Georgie looked from him to the dripping faucet. It was now more of a spurt, and getting stronger. "Can you fix it?"

"Reckon we can." He hefted his toolbox. "Better get to it."

Not British, she thought. Some country way down south. Australia or Africa. Or maybe New Zealand. "Thanks for saving me from a nosedive."

"You're welcome." He headed off to join his partner, and said over his shoulder, "We'll be turning the water off for a while, so you'd better fill the kettle if you want a cuppa."

"Sure." She looked at the rapidly spreading puddle, inching its way toward her trailer, and sighed. This was like the Wild West when women dragged their long skirts through muddy streets while dodging bullets. Well, not that people were shooting at her, but her skirt *was* too long.

Note to self, she thought, next time take the hem up *before* going up and down steps and through the mud.

Fighting down the urge to tuck the skirt up into her underwear as she had done as a child, she picked up a basket and went to retrieve her washing.

Soon it would be happy hour when everyone

congregated to have a coffee or a drink and talk. And to chat about road trips.

She planned to be there, in her new gypsy gear, talking about her wonderful gypsy trailer.

Twenty-two sales to go.

CHAPTER 6

A Plea for Help

The next morning Georgie was up bright and early, packing up the array of hoses, cables, her clothesline, and all the other bits and pieces. Being on the road full-time in a vintage RV was, she discovered, quite a bit more involved than taking one to an RV show for a couple of days. Still, she had to admit she liked it. There was something nice about waking up to a park full of friendly people who took life at a relaxed pace.

There was something nice about not having to turn up to an office every day, too. Even if her father owned that office, and wasn't too concerned if she was late for work.

She coiled the gray water hose and stowed it in

the nifty little compartment that her father had made for it, and then took a moment to stand back to gaze at the sky. It was a perfect day to be driving anywhere. The sky was completely blue, with just a hint of fluffy clouds in the distance. With only 70 miles to go to the Columbus vintage rally, she would make it in plenty of time to set up and have a chance to check out the other exhibitors before the crowds arrived the next day.

And the crazy retro/vintage crew would be there early in full force, ready to party, which would make it even more fun. Quite a number of them had bought their trailers from her.

Sliding into the seat of the truck, she edged it forward and then used a combination of the rear sensors and the side mirrors to get it into position. She was conscious of several men standing nearby watching and was half expecting them to come up and offer her a hand. Most men, she had discovered, didn't expect a woman to be able to back a car in and hitch up a travel trailer.

They didn't know that Georgie B. Goode had been backing trucks onto trailers practically since she was old enough to get a license. Johnny had made certain that both his children could do any task they needed to in the RV yard, while the business was growing through its various phases.

With quick, economical movements, she wound up the stabilizer legs, hitched up the trailer, and checked that the entire rig was riding level. It should be. Her father was a stickler for weight distribution, and she'd had to be able to talk to customers in their language. She stood back and regarded it with a critical eye. Yes, even Johnny would have to admit that was as straight as a die.

"I can see you've done this before."

The Australian or African or New Zealand accent told her who it was before she even turned around: her knight in gardening clothes from the day before. Georgie turned around and smiled at him, gesturing at her jeans. "Yep. Getting ready to hit the road. I've ditched the skirt for something more practical."

"Practical, but not as decorative." He walked along the side of her trailer, checking it out. "Nice unit. You've got the vintage look, but I can see that it's been made to travel the highways. Right?"

She nodded. "Right. My dad would have nothing less. Every RV he makes can be towed along the highway at the same speed as other vehicles. It's not unusual for people who start off buying a pre-loved trailer to give up and come to us for the look and feel of vintage, without the problems. We copy the structure, but everything's compliant." Georgie smiled, hearing herself. "Sorry. Didn't mean to give you the sales talk."

He grinned back at her, a move that deepened the laughter lines around his eyes. "When you say 'we'…" He gestured towards Jerry's silver motorhome a few sites away. "You're one of the Johnny B. Goode RV Empire people?"

Georgie made a wry face and stuck out her hand. "Georgie B. Goode at your service. No doubt you'll have seen my dad on TV ads."

He shook her hand. "I thought so. I'm Scott." He looked at Jerry's RV again. "I was weeding the flowerbeds when your other salesman was working the crowd yesterday morning. You didn't look too happy. Bit of competition there?"

"That was my brother, Jerry. Competitive is not the word. Try 'win at any cost'. I want to handle the vintage trailer section of the business. So does Jerry. He's quite prepared to steal a sale out from under my nose."

"And he did?"

"He tried." She showed her teeth. "Let's say I outwitted him."

He nodded and then waved to the other gardener who was waiting next to a half-built aviary a few hundred yards away and giving him hurry-up signs. "Gotta go. So, where to now?"

"The vintage rally over near Columbus. Should be a good opportunity to make a few more sales."

"Safe travels, then." He looked back at the gypsy trailer, gleaming in the morning sun. "Can I ask you something?"

"Sure."

"I've heard some talk around the RV Park…. Are you really telling fortunes, or is that just a bit of showmanship to make the trailer look more authentic?"

It sounded like Kaylene had been passing the word. For a moment Georgie debated how to answer that one. *Did* she tell fortunes? The answer was undoubtedly "not very well."

"I'm kind of new to it," she finally said. "My great-grandmother is the real deal. She seems to think that I'm the one to inherit her crown, so to speak—but I don't know. I guess I'm going to have to find out."

"It's my day off tomorrow. I might drive up to

the rally and come see you; have my fortune told. You up for it?"

"Well, uh—" Georgie was a little taken aback. "I'm not promising anything…"

"I've got to see one of the manufacturers in Columbus anyway, about a problem with my RV. And since my mother used to do readings, I'm kind of interested."

"Your *mother*?" Intrigued, Georgie stared at him. "She reads a crystal ball?"

"Not that kind of reading. She—"

The sound of quick footsteps behind them had them both turning. Georgie's heart sank. It was Kaylene.

"I'm sorry, I can see you're hitching up to leave. I was just wondering--do you have time to talk to me for just a moment? Please?"

Georgie looked at her more closely. Kaylene's eyes were red, as though she'd been crying, and then hastily washed her face. She glanced uneasily at the gardener next to her. "Gosh, I don't know, Kaylene. I kind of don't have a lot of time – I'm a little later getting away than I expected, and I've got to make it to the vintage rally over in Columbus this morning." She hesitated, torn. She didn't want to get involved with whatever was going on in Kaylene's world. On the other hand, she was the one who had told her to listen to her gut.

"Well, if you'll excuse me, I'd better get to work or they'll decide not to pay me." Scott nodded at both of them. "I'll see you tomorrow, maybe." He headed off towards the aviary.

While Georgie hesitated, wondering what to say, Kaylene decided for her. "Sorry. I know what it's like when you're trying to get away, and someone comes up to talk. I'll tell you what—if I drive up to the rally tomorrow, can you fit me in?"

First Scott, now Kaylene again. This fortune-telling thing was running away on her. She'd better figure it out fast. Georgie thought quickly. Would it be better to see Kaylene here, and get away a little late? Then the roar of a motorhome engine distracted her for a moment, and Jerry slowly rolled by, tooting and giving her an exaggerated wave.

No, she had to get going. Knowing Jerry, he would grab a suitably central position and start priming people before she even got there. Then he'd tell them to ask his sister to show them the trailer and come back to him for a special deal.

No way.

"But maybe you're just going there to sell trailers?" Kaylene said, sounding both disappointed and desperate.

Georgie gave in. "Tomorrow would be great, Kaylene," she said. "What time do you think you'll get there? I'll watch out for you."

"I'll leave here by eight-thirty. Say around 10 AM?"

"Fine."

"Thank you. Thank you so much. Darryl, he —" Kaylene hesitated. "I kind of let out that I'd been to see you. I told him what you said and he said he had no idea who this Brian was, unless you meant Brian Payne. He didn't say all *that* much, but I could see he was offended. Then I felt bad. Anyway…I'll see you tomorrow, OK?"

"Fine." Instinctively, Georgie reached out and seized Kaylene's hand in both of hers. "Hang in there, Kaylene. You've got to make up your own mind, not let him get you so confused you don't know what to think. Just think it through, and I'll see you tomorrow."

"Thank you. So much!" Kaylene looked marginally happier. "Well, I'll let you get on with things."

Georgie stared after her as she hurried away, and then looked down at her hands. They were tingling, both of them. And she had a bad feeling about Kaylene.

Rosa's words came back to her, echoing through the years. "It doesn't matter what you use. The Sight comes from the same place."

What kind of switch had she flipped when she first looked into that crystal ball?

CHAPTER 7

Fake It 'til You Make It

That afternoon, Georgie was welcomed into the vintage-and-retro crowd like one of their own. "Georgie! Over here!" was a common cry, as was "Come and see what I've done with the trailer you sold me!"

She popped in and out of RVs, her grin growing wider by the moment. This segment of the RV industry was taking off; there were hundreds of retro trailers here.

Oh yeah, she *loved* vintage and retro. These were her people!

As the sun went down and she joined a large group around a campfire, wine glass in hand, the questions got more personal.

"How come you're not traveling in a motorhome like last year?"

"Love your outfit, Georgie!"

"Do the Goodes really come from gypsy stock like your Dad says on TV?"

"Is that crystal ball for real? Can you tell my fortune?"

She fended the questions adroitly (because I love vintage, yes I do have a Gypsy heritage, yes the crystal ball is real and I'll tell your fortune tomorrow!) That last was said with her fingers crossed since she still felt like a fraud.

Jerry made a point of dropping by, of course. He worked the crowd diligently at every RV show or rally.

"Hey, Sis!" he dropped a kiss on the top of her head and solicitously tucked the bright embroidered shawl more closely around her shoulders. "Enjoy your trip?"

"Great, thanks." Her cool tone said: *Go away, Jerry.*

"Have you all seen inside Georgie's Vardo?" At the chorus of yeses he went on, "Didn't she do a brilliant job with the interior design? She's got great taste."

He sounded genuinely proud and interested, the jerk. Georgie reached up to pat the hand resting on her shoulder and managed to stab him with a diamond-hard fingernail. "You're too kind, Jerry."

He withdrew the hand hastily but didn't miss a beat. "Don't forget we'll work with any of you to get exactly what you want. Bow-top or Vardo trailer, or a customized retro design for any decade—feel free to talk to me or Georgie over the weekend." He waved a hand casually. "You all know where to find Georgie, but I'm in the silver Johnny B. Goode motorhome right down near the stalls and displays. Come and see me at any time, day or night."

With the emphasis on 'night', Georgie thought, not failing to notice the admiring looks from a couple of the younger females.

Judging her tolerance level perfectly, Jerry winked at her and went on his merry way.

"That's kind of him," said a vivacious blonde called Tammy, running a finger over her scarlet lips and crossing her knees. She was clad in tight 50s-style pedal pushers and a fitted shirt, which showed off her impressive figure to advantage. "I'm in the market for a smaller trailer. I don't know whether to stay 50s retro or go gypsy." She grinned at Georgie. "Why do you sometimes call it a caravan?"

"They're called caravans in Europe and Australia," Georgie said. "I think it suits them."

Layla, a dark-haired girl sitting next to her, leaned over and said to Georgie in a low voice, "Tell me to butt out if I'm being rude, but do you get a commission for each sale? Or doesn't it count because you're family?"

"We get the same commission as everyone else," Georgie said. Then she had an inspiration, and whispered back, "But, confidentially, Jerry and I are going head to head at the moment. I'd like to beat him. So pass the word, will you?"

"Got it." Layla winked and clinked glasses.

Georgie could hardly believe her daring.

She was becoming as devious as Jerry.

The next morning, Georgie ate breakfast at her laptop while she guiltily did a Google search for *How to Read a Crystal Ball.*

Crystal balls, she discovered, could be made of glass, crystal, or quartz. Who would have thought? Rosa hadn't passed on that information.

She kept skimming web pages, keeping one eye on the time, and frowned. Was she supposed to cleanse the ball of any previous energy by smudging it with sage? Rosa hadn't said anything about that

—unless she'd done it herself before handing it over. If she hadn't, did that mean it was full of *Rosa's* energy?

That could be a good thing, since her great-granddaughter didn't have much idea of what she was doing. With luck, some of Rosa's wisdom might be hanging around the crystal. (Or quartz, or glass.) She read on. She was supposed to gaze into the crystal ball, focus on what she wanted to know, and zone out. Well, she had kind of done that before she got Brian's name, whoever he might be. Which didn't appear to be much help to poor Kaylene. The thought of her very first customer ever made her glance at her watch. Kaylene would be here in a couple of hours, seeking more insights.

Help.

She switched to Internet sites on reading palms and tea leaves, just in case anyone asked. There was a handy palm chart, which she could use as a reference if she printed it off. But not today. The crystal ball was enough of a challenge.

Tea leaves…Georgie frowned, turning her head on the side to view sample tea leaf spreads. Apart from a few blobs that did look like something, most of the examples on the screen looked like…well, wet tea leaves.

I am *so* not cut out for this, she thought in a mild panic.

Fake it till you make it.

At eight-thirty she gave up and took her laptop back outside to the sales tent next to her trailer. The whole thing was due to kick off at nine.

Georgie arranged and re-arranged the colorful brochures featuring all kinds of retro trailers and double-checked that her wireless terminal was working so she could take credit card deposits. She printed a sign saying:

Georgie (8th Generation Gypsy)
Fortunes Told 10 am, 12 pm, 2 pm

Then she realized that telling fortunes would mean that the sales tent would be unattended during those times, so she carefully hand-lettered another saying:

Back in one hour!

Jerry would sneer at such inefficiency. He would have *fired* any sales assistant that didn't stay at the sales table for the entire day.

Dammit. She should have thought of hiring an

assistant. Jerry would undoubtedly be hovering around, ready to jump in and corral her customers if she wasn't around.

Double dammit.

Then Layla came along and saved her. She breezed up twenty minutes before the gates were due to open, read the signs, and summed up the situation immediately.

"Who's standing in for you when you're reading fortunes?" and then, reading Georgie's expression, nodded and answered herself. "Nobody."

"I didn't think," Georgie said.

"Your brother—"

"—will come along and take the sales. I know." Georgie sighed.

"Not if I can help it," Layla said decisively. "Sarah and Jack are coming to talk to you about upgrading to a bigger trailer. Sixties era, like their old one. I've had a word, and they'll go through you, not Jerry."

Georgie hugged her impulsively. "Thank you! That's so generous of you."

Layla laughed. "I've got an ulterior motive. I want my fortune told. Can I be your first appointment if I get one of the girls to mind the booth?"

"Sorry, I've got someone driving here from

Dayton for the ten o'clock," Georgie said apologetically. "I thought twenty minutes for each one." She hesitated for a moment. "Unless you want to do it now?"

"Done." Layla pointed at the printed notice. "I'd put your prices on here if I were you. People like to know what they're paying before they commit."

Georgie hadn't been planning on charging anything, since she was still learning the ropes. "I hadn't planned on charging anything," she said hesitantly. "I thought, like, a Johnny B. Goode RV Show Special—fortunes told free…?"

"Nonsense," Layla said. "You have to charge *something*. OK, let's do it, and then we'll talk about what price you should put on it."

Georgie blinked. Johnny B. Goode's RV Empire could use take-charge salespeople like Layla. She'd be an excellent on-road contact.

Hmmm. *Now there's a thought.* She filed it away for later and led Layla inside for her second-ever crystal ball reading.

"I just so love this trailer," Layla said, gazing around enviously. She flipped her ebony shoulder-length hair over her shoulder, her dark eyes flitting from one feature to another. "Just look at that darling little carved bird, peeking out from the corner of the shelf."

"Thank you," Georgie said, pleased. "That was my suggestion." She gave the crystal ball a surreptitious wipe as she removed Rosa's velvet cloth, and then put it on the table and closed the door, so the interior of the trailer was dim. For the final touch, she lit a candle and placed it on the shelf.

"Is there anything you especially want to know about?" she asked, lifting the ball in her hands for a moment.

Imagine yourself at one with the crystal ball…

(At one with Rosa? That was a scary thought.)

Concentrate, Georgie.

"Well, I'm not prepared for this," said Layla, "but I guess I have been wondering what I should do with my life. My family is a bit impatient with me. They think I should settle down and…well, do something 'useful'. Maybe you can just tell me what you see in store for me?"

"OK." Georgie sucked her bottom lip between her teeth, concentrating, and gently placed the ball back on its ornate base. She stared into it. It was still clear… but she could feel a warm sort of tingle.

That was interesting. Unless she was just getting panicky.

Concentrate!

Then the crystal ball seemed to dull slightly, and the white mist slowly filled it.

Georgie's heartbeat slowed.

On one level she was thinking, *Hey, this is working*, and on another, she was kind of…opening up.

"You should travel," she said slowly. "Start by heading east. That's where you'll find opportunity." She felt compelled to add: "Niagara Falls."

"East?" Layla had been staring at the ball, but her head came up. "That's weird. I was looking at maps last night. Right before bed. And I *circled* Niagara Falls." She sent Georgie a strange look. "And I didn't talk about it when we were all together, either."

Georgie barely paid attention, as words filled her mind. "You already know where you should go, what to do." So weird: all she was doing was passing on messages. It was almost as easy as reading it out of a book. "You've thought about this. You just need reassurance that you're doing the right thing."

"Will I…find somebody?"

"Not right away." *How can I know that?* "You'll meet people, but it will take a while to find the right one. Just enjoy yourself."

"I had planned to," said Layla with a wicked grin.

Georgie heard herself say: "In California. That's where you'll commit to someone. Eventually." She glanced at Layla and sat back, shocked. Where had that come from? Then even more words spilled from her lips. "You've just terminated a relationship with… Danny. No, Davy. Davy?" Suddenly she was unsure of herself, looking at Layla for confirmation.

Layla's eyebrows shot up. "His parents called him David. I called him Davy, and they hated it." She gave a somewhat forlorn smile. "They hated me too. Too bohemian for them. He was only going out with me as an act of rebellion, so I called it quits. He didn't seem too broken up about it."

"But you were."

"Yes, I was." She gave her shoulders a shake. "But that's over and done. Do you see anything else?"

Surprisingly, Georgie did. Small things, most of them, but…accurate. The minutes flew by until the sound of approaching voices had them both checking their watches.

"It's after nine! Here they come." Layla put her hand on Georgie's. "Thank you—seriously. You are good at this, aren't you? But you have to charge; people will expect it."

"You choose, then. Just write something on the notice." Quickly, Georgie covered Rosa's crystal ball and blew out the candle, and followed Layla outside, with a brief backward glance and one last thought.

Maybe Rosa's crystal ball really would become *her* crystal ball.

CHAPTER 8

Unfinished Business

Georgie sifted through the pile of brochures until she found the one she wanted. "Here you are, Connie—I think this one would be perfect for you. A brand new retro trailer in the Vagabond style: it's lightweight with a super-easy hitch, and the exact colors you wanted—what do you think?" With a beaming smile, she turned the brochure around so Connie could have a look at it.

Connie, a woman in her early sixties with a long grey braid down her back and sun-worn skin, didn't need to say anything: her gasp of delight and the hand that flew to her mouth said it all. She had suspicious brightness in her eyes. Georgie smiled. "Lovely, isn't it?"

Connie took a moment to compose herself, and

then drew the brochure closer. "This is perfect, Georgie. This is exactly like the one my mother had—the one that we traveled around in when I was little." She hesitated a moment, studying the specifications. "How much will this cost? With all the inclusions we were talking about?"

Georgie thought swiftly. Connie obviously didn't have a lot of savings, and she didn't mind knocking down her commission a bit. Heck, she was having so much fun, she didn't mind if she got no commission at all. She mentally rolled her eyes, imagining what Jerry would think of that idea.

"Connie, how about you let me crunch some numbers on this, and get back to you. I promise I'll do the very best deal I can."

By then Connie had spotted the recommended retail figure, and she didn't say anything for a moment, obviously weighing up her options. Then she gave a short, sharp nod. "You know what? My house is on the market, and I'm going to live with the kids anyway, sharing my time around—when I'm not on the road, that is. I know you'll do me a good deal, Georgie, but I'm going to have it anyway! How much deposit do you need?"

Georgie laid a hand on Connie's wrinkled wrist. "How about a hundred dollars?"

"A hundred dollars? Not five percent?"

Georgie winked. "Special deal for you, Connie."

"And you did say that air conditioning is included? Not as an extra?"

"All included, Connie." Georgie leaned over and pointed at the cunningly hidden air conditioning vents in the interior shot. "Hidden behind these carvings. We try to keep it all as faithful to the original as possible while giving you all modern conveniences and still meeting code."

"Can I keep this? I want to show my children."

"You bet." Georgie rapidly walked Connie through the order form, and then turned the page around and presented her with the pen. "There you are, Connie. Your brand-new 1960s retro-look trailer. You'll be able to travel in this comfortably for many years—and have a wonderful time."

Connie signed with a flourish, her grin as wide as the sky. "And you know what? I'm going to come back to this rally every year, and join in all the fun. You'll see me at every vintage trailer show around the country."

"I'll be looking forward to it." Georgie dug into the hamper sitting at her feet. She drew out a gift-wrapped parcel, and a bottle of sparkling wine.

"And here's a celebration treat for you, Connie. Enjoy!"

"Thank you! I'll save that for our get-together tonight." Connie looked around and realized that several people were waiting to sit down and discuss things with Georgie. "I'd better let someone else have a turn. Make sure you come over and visit, mind? You have to celebrate with me."

"I'll do that for sure." Georgie smiled and then looked up to nod at the next person in line. "Hi. What can I help you with today?" She slid Connie's paperwork in the folder with the others and became immersed in the next round of questions.

The first hour passed in a flash, and before she knew it Layla was nudging her and pointing to the small queue waiting at the steps to her trailer, most of who were sending covert glances her way. "I think you've got a few customers waiting."

"Are you sure you can handle this by yourself?"

"Go do your duty. I'll be fine." Layla gave her a cheerful dig with her elbow. "I worked in the hospitality industry long enough to learn how to keep people happy while they wait." She glanced at the hamper of goodies on the floor. "You don't mind if I give people a voucher for a free coffee while they're waiting?"

"Of course not." Convinced that she was leaving things in good hands, even though she felt a bit guilty, Georgie stood up and moved across to her gypsy trailer.

Kaylene was at the head of the queue.

"Hi, Kaylene. Right on time! Glad you could make it." She nodded cheerfully at the others. "Each session is about twenty minutes. I can book you all a slot now if you like. Just give me your name and a contact number, in case you don't make it back for your appointment."

Wow, she thought, already she had enough people to fill this hour and the next one starting at midday. What had she started?

As soon as she'd taken names, she and Kaylene moved inside and closed the door.

"Sit down." She nodded at the seat and whisked the black cloth off the crystal ball. Even though she'd done only two readings, this time she felt a little less panicky—as long as she could come up with something definite for Kaylene.

Kaylene sat down. "I feel as though I'm wasting your time. Darryl's been so patient, and he even showed me his driver's license and credit card to prove that he was who he said he was. I feel guilty, now, coming to ask you about him."

Georgie didn't know quite what to say for a moment. Telling Kaylene that the Goode RV Empire had encountered lots of people with fake IDs didn't seem tactful, so she just nodded and cupped the crystal ball in her hands, staring at it intently. After a few moments she said, "Kaylene, whatever it was that made you come to me in the first place, you can't lose anything by being careful. I'm not going to try to force you into anything—or talk you out of anything. OK?"

Kaylene relaxed a little. "OK."

Georgie gently set the crystal ball down in its stand and waited. This time, she didn't feel her skin grow warmer as she had in this morning's session with Layla. If anything, she seemed to cool down. *Strange.* Obviously, you couldn't count on the same conditions twice.

She focused on the question in her mind: *Is Darryl the right person for Kaylene? Does she have anything to worry about?* She kept her gaze on the crystal ball and felt a quick surge of relief when the white mist began to swirl in its depths. Much as she looked, she couldn't see any images, but the feeling that crept over her was unmistakable. It wasn't exactly a shiver that went up her spine, but more a slow, curling sense of wrongness.

"Can you see anything?" Kaylene's voice was tentative, and Georgie looked up to see the other woman watching her face.

"Kaylene…." It was so hard to know how to put this. She didn't want to ruin someone's life based on a *feeling*.

Then it came again. *Brian*…

Georgie gave a little sigh, and sat back, looking from the crystal ball to Kaylene. "I still keep getting that name, Kaylene. Brian. *Brian*." She shrugged and held her hands out wide. "Let's talk about Darryl's family. He hasn't got a brother or father named Brian? A friend named Brian? *Anyone* you should be concerned about?"

Kaylene's head shake was decisive. "No. Definitely not. We went through this whole Brian thing and I asked the same questions, and he can't think of a single person. The only Brian we both know is the one three sites away from us back at the RV park. Brian Payne. I told you about him."

"Hmm." Georgie thought for a moment, her mind going down another track. Could it be that the mysterious Brian was the man Kaylene was destined to marry if she just waited? Her soulmate, maybe.

Perhaps she shouldn't sell up and move in with Darryl because the man who *was* right for her was waiting in the wings?

She waited, turning that thought over, but if she was expecting a blinding flash of revelation (*Yes! That's it! She has to wait for a Brian in her life!*), she was going to be disappointed.

The crystal ball was being no help at all. She decided to approach the whole puzzle from a different angle. "Then let's forget it for the moment, and we'll focus on the men in your past. See if we can come at it from another direction."

Kaylene was happy to go along with that, and over the next few minutes, Georgie got a very good picture of what the girl had been through in the last ten years. Talk about a battler—poor Kaylene didn't seem to be able to take a trick. Pregnant in her last year of school, held at arm's distance by her family until she miscarried, and then conned or mistreated by a succession of men after that—no wonder she was man-shy.

Finally, the session was finished, and Kaylene stood up, with no new insights at all. "I can see my time is up. Thanks, Georgie." Reading Georgie's frustration, she added: "It's been nice talking with you about this, even if we've got nothing definite to go on. I'll give this serious thought, but I have to make a decision soon—Darryl's had a job offer in Pennsylvania, and we need to get on the road."

Disaster, Georgie thought bleakly. But without anything concrete to offer Kaylene, what could she say?

"Be careful." Georgie gave her one of her Johnny B. Goode business cards. "Call me if you get worried, OK?"

She watched her walk away. Kaylene Waters, she felt certain, was unfinished business—but she simply didn't have time to sort it out now.

CHAPTER 9

Who's Leo?

By the time everyone packed up their booths that afternoon, Georgie was exhausted. She slid into the seat next to Layla and groaned. "My head is spinning. Going into people's heads all day is like digging ditches." When Layla laughed, she flapped a hand. "No, really. Mentally, I feel as though I've done ten rounds in a boxing ring." She eyed the pile of papers in front of the other girl. "So, how'd we do?"

"Lots of fish nibbling at the bait, but they're all looking for the best deal. There are five different distributors of vintage and retro RVs here, did you know? We have made two sales, though. One was Connie—what a darling!—and the other was to a nice young couple who are getting rid of their big modern trailer to buy a Vardo just like yours."

"That last one was all thanks to you. Thanks so much, Layla. Honestly, I don't know what I would have done if you hadn't come along." Georgie popped the tab on a cool drink.

Layla nudged her. "Have a look over there. Tammy didn't waste any time taking your brother up on his offer." Georgie's eyes followed Layla's pointing finger, and she had to laugh. There was Tammy, clad in a full polka-dot skirt and a bright 50s blouse, carrying on an animated conversation while she walked along beside Jerry. She was carrying a large stack of brochures, and they were heading in the direction of the RV Empire motorhome.

Georgie sent Layla a sideways look. "Did Jerry happen to come by earlier when you were manning the table?"

"Yep. He even stopped to talk and ask how you were doing. I played dumb, said I was just taking names while you were busy." Layla looked down at her 50s-style casual clothes. "He commented on how my outfit was the right look for selling retro trailers. You think that inspired him to recruit Tammy to do the same thing?"

"Of course it did. He's always in recruitment mode anyway: we have a road team for all the different RVs we sell—people who are traveling all the time and love the lifestyle." Georgie watched the bright red-and-white skirt disappear into the crowds. "You saw last night what a fun rockabilly-type girl Tammy is. Looking like that, she'll draw the crowds. Dammit. That'll boost his sales figures again."

"I wonder if she spent the night with him?" mused Layla, her eyes sparkling. "Your brother does seem the type to take advantage of all benefits." Then she cast Georgie a quick look. "Oops, hope I'm not treading on toes here. I shouldn't be casting aspersions on your family."

Georgie laughed. "You're not the first, I assure you."

"Hey there," a cheerful voice broke in. "Got time to tell one more fortune?"

Georgie glanced up. "Scott! You did make it."

He pulled up a spare chair and leaned back, looking relaxed in his cargo pants and t-shirt. "Said I would. Got held up though back at the RV park… plumbing problems; the faucet on your site was just the start of it. I didn't get away until two. And then I had to see the guy in Columbus about repairs to my RV before they closed up for the day." He looked at Georgie, his warm brown eyes concerned. "I saw Kaylene before I left. She said she came to see you this morning."

"Yes. I wasn't much help, unfortunately." She realized that Scott might be just the person to help her. "Tell me, what do you know about Brian Payne?"

"The bloke in the bus with the bad paint job?" Scott took his time to consider, then gave his verdict in two words. "Pretty harmless."

Georgie frowned. "Harmless? What do you mean?"

"Just that." Scott shrugged. "Works part-time at the packaging plant in town. He walks around the park a bit, talking to everyone who rolls in. A bit lonely, I'd say."

"He isn't making a nuisance of himself with Kaylene? Hasn't been acting strangely?"

"Not that I've noticed."

Georgie let out a huff of frustration. "Well, that's my last hope. There's no other Brian."

"When I left she was busy packing up." Scott's forehead was creased, and from the look in his eyes, she could tell he was as concerned as she was. "She says they're heading out tomorrow."

Layla pushed back her chair, stood up, and stretched. "I might go back to my trailer now if you don't need me for anything else?"

"Hardly. You've worked hard enough." Georgie raised a tired fist and they bumped knuckles. "Thanks again. I'll be over for a quick visit after dinner."

They both watched her go, and then Scott said: "You don't have to tell my fortune. You must need a break by now if you've been at it all day. I just wanted to call in and say hello."

Georgie was tempted to agree and go and put her feet up, but she was curious about his mother. And he had come all this way. Besides, she liked him. He cared about people.

"No, that's all right. You can be my last customer for the day. Come on."

Unlike her brother Jerry, whose words had managed to make her beloved trailer seem small and uncomfortable, Scott looked around approvingly as soon as he walked through the door. "Nice. Homey." He leaned closer to examine some of the carving on the outside ledge of the shelves. "Good workmanship here. Is this standard, or did you commission this?"

"I drew pictures of what I wanted, and collected

photos of other trailers that had touches I wanted." Delighted at his interest, Georgie walked him around the Vardo trailer, pointing out the clever touches that made the most of storage in a small space.

Finally, she lit the candle and they sat at the small table. "You seem to know a lot about cabinetry. About RVs, actually. Did you do some work in that line?" she asked, automatically picking up the crystal ball to let its energy flow through her.

"I've turned my hand to most things. I've worked in National Parks and Fisheries—but I've built and repaired fences, huts, that kind of thing."

"Where? Africa? Australia? I can't quite make out your accent."

"Australia first, then over here. Right now I'm seeing the country before going back home. I'm just picking up odd jobs here and there—like two months at the RV Park in Dayton."

The sound of his voice was soothing, like warm honey. A nice way to finish the day, she thought. Most people today seemed to have some pressing problem they wanted answers for. Not Scott—or it didn't appear so.

The crystal ball in her hands was completely clear.

No mist. She looked up and smiled at him. "It seems my crystal ball has gone to sleep for the night. Nothing." Then, just as she said it, a flicker in the ball caught her eye. She glanced back at it and frowned. *Rosa?*

"What is it?" He leaned forward, interested. "I can't see anything."

Nor could she, now, but she could have sworn she saw—for the fraction of a second—her great-grandmother's face; grinning widely at her, all pink gums and large teeth.

Georgie couldn't be bothered fibbing. "There's nothing to see now, but I thought I saw my great-grandmother's face. Just a blink. Maybe I'm seeing things."

"Your great-grandmother? The one who gave you the crystal ball?"

"Yes." She gave herself a mental shake. "So, how do you want to do this? Just see what I can pick up about you?" She smiled ruefully. "I probably shouldn't have asked all those questions about you first. Isn't that what the shysters always do?"

He looked sympathetic. "My mother had a lot of people accuse her of that. She was fairly philosophical about it; she believed in what she could see." His gaze was back on the crystal ball. "She always told me not to force it. If it's going to come, she said, it will come without effort." In answer to Georgie's questioning look, he went on, "She was into astrology. Read the cards, did astrological charts for people. What's your star sign?"

"Me? Libra."

He hesitated, then appeared to make a decision. "She told me I'd meet you."

Open-mouthed, Georgie stared at him. "She did? What did she say?"

"That I'd meet a dark-haired Libra, across the ocean. Someone who had the Sight, passed down through generations." He raised a finger. "However, she did get the color of the trailer wrong. White, she said. With carved flowers."

"I was looking at one like that, to begin with." Georgie caught another flicker in the crystal ball and stole a sideways glance.

It *was* Rosa. What was she up to?

Then the words came into her mind, as clear as the moment Rosa had uttered them, just a few days before. *Say hello to your Leo.*

Who's Leo? Georgie had called out.

Realization hit. "What star sign are you?"

"Leo," he said. "Aquarius rising. If my mother is correct, your birthday should be early in October."

He quirked an eyebrow. "According to her, our paths will cross more than once. I don't know what *you* have to say about that."

Stunned, Georgie had nothing to say.

But she could feel Rosa's amusement.

CHAPTER 10

Just Like Speed Dating...

The next day, Sunday, visitors flooded into the rally, delighted at the opportunity to inspect the vintage trailers. Georgie and Layla fell into an easy rhythm, with Layla staying at the sales tent to help out throughout the day. Everything seemed to work. The small pile of order forms grew, and with Jerry's *there are no rules* in mind, Georgie scanned each one and sent it through to head office immediately.

"Seven," she said with satisfaction, riffling through the orders one last time before packing up. "That's nine for the weekend. Not bad for a rally, especially with competitors here."

Layla's competitive spirit was in high rev. "How many so far for the month?"

"Twelve. Still 14 to go." Georgie calculated the days left in the month since the day she had agreed to the targets set by her father. "From here I need to sell nearly one a day." She felt the sharp pang of disappointment. "That won't be easy. At a rally like this, people visit *wanting* to buy. It's different on the road."

"Where are you going next?"

"I thought I'd mosey on up to Niagara Falls; there'll be plenty of tourists. Get the Vardo in front of as many eyes as possible."

Layla toyed with a pile of brochures. "I don't suppose you want company?"

Georgie stared at her. "You're kidding. Really?"

"I've been thinking. You said the business has a road team." Layla kept her voice calm, but Georgie could hear the underlying hope. "I've been looking for something I can do that's not waiting tables or cleaning hotel rooms. And I think I'm good at this." She waved a hand in the general direction of the cluster of vintage trailers. "I travel in a retro trailer. My parents think that's crazy, but I love it. I was thinking, maybe I could be a regular part of your team." She sat forward. "Just on trial to begin with, maybe? What do you think?"

"On trial?" Georgie laughed, giddy with excitement. "What do you think this weekend has been? You're *great* at this. I'll make sure you get the commission from all the ones you've sold so far."

"Oh no, you don't need to do that. That's not why I suggested it."

"I know it isn't," Georgie said, "but I'm going to do it anyway. Fair's fair. Welcome to the team."

"*Georgie!* Thanks so much!" Layla's face was alight with pleasure.

Things were falling into place, thought Georgie. With Layla's help, she might have a chance.

Then she looked up and saw Jerry striding her way. Tammy was trotting along beside him, laughing and gesturing, as animated as always.

Tammy looked great, Georgie had to admit. She had the whole 50s rock and roll thing going on, with a black and white polka dot swing skirt appliquéd with big pink musical notes, a body-hugging pink shirt, and a black and white polka dot necktie. And black ballet slip-ons.

And the bangs, with hair cinched up in a chic little ponytail that bobbed as she walked.

Customers would be attracted to her like bees to honey.

"Here we go," she warned Layla, her mood instantly plunging. "Salesman of the Year is here with our rockabilly girl. He's probably already reached his target for the month."

The two of them sashayed up, grinning. "Hey, Sis," Jerry greeted her cheerfully and nodded at Layla. "So, how'd you do?"

"Nine," she said, knowing that he'd be able to check the sales figures online anyway. "Five retro and four gypsy. And you?"

He looked superior. "Tammy, since you did so much of the work, would you like to do the honors?"

"*Ten*," she said with a happy smile, holding up a folder full of forms. "Eight retro, two gypsy. Including the new one I ordered for myself. Jerry did me such a good deal on it, I couldn't believe it. I can't wait!"

Ten. Georgie felt deflated. She'd thought with the added hook of telling fortunes, and Layla at her side, she would beat him.

It wasn't fair. She *should* be the one running the division. She forced a smile anyway. "Congratulations. But the month isn't over yet. What's your overall total?"

His smile changed from triumph into something more predatory. "Eleven. So you're ahead on points. You'd be up to twelve, right?"

"Right."

"As you say, the month isn't over yet." He put an arm around Tammy's shoulders. "And I have a new secret weapon. Say hello to the newest member of our road team!"

Georgie smiled sweetly at Tammy. "How wonderful." She kicked Layla, warning her to be quiet. Let Jerry think he had the advantage. She wouldn't tell him any more than she had to. "Welcome aboard, Tammy. If you're selling retro, we'll be in touch quite a bit about design. And," she added generously, "I can see you're a great advertisement for the lifestyle."

"Thanks," Tammy said. "I might need to talk to you soon. Some of our customers are picky about the interior."

Tell me about it, Georgie thought. Wait until Tammy encountered a few of the Customers from Hell. That might take some of the shine off it. She focused on Jerry again, pasting a resigned look on her face. "Nice move. Adding Tammy to your team is going to make it far more of a challenge for me, isn't it?"

"That's what it's all about." Annoyingly, he flicked her nose. "No rules, Georgie."

"No rules," she echoed. "Well, we'd better pack up. Are you staying for happy hour?"

"No. Back to home base for me; too much work to do tomorrow."

Tammy looked disappointed and turned to him. "Do you have to go right away?"

Jerry hesitated, and Georgie could see the wheels turning. Best not to alienate his new secret weapon when he needed the sales. "Well, maybe not right away. I'll stay for an hour or so. But then I do have to go. I've got paperwork to do tonight, and a customer coming for his new RV at 7:30. He insists I walk him through it."

"An hour's better than nothing." Tammy tugged at his arm. "Come on, then—let's not waste any of it."

They watched the two walk towards the RV campground and then exchanged speaking looks.

"You're not telling him about me?" Layla said. "*Your* secret weapon?" She made a face. "Of course, I can't measure up to Tammy. Just look at her."

"You did just fine," Georgie said. "And no, I'm not telling him about you for now. The less he knows the better. Let's pack up and go and socialize." She grinned. "Keep an eye out for any more prospects for *our* road team. This is war."

At the social get-together, it was clear that Tammy was more than a little interested in Georgie's handsome brother. What Georgie found intriguing, though, was that he seemed to be increasingly drawn to her, too. Georgie had watched Jerry-the-smooth-operator in action for years, and even when he had appeared to be devoting all his attention to his latest acquisition, she could tell that he held part of himself back.

That wasn't the feeling she was getting this time.

Tammy was popular. She was interested in everything, and had a quick wit, turning some of Jerry's teasing back on him in a flash. Perhaps that was part of the appeal, Georgie thought. It would do Jerry good to have someone who would challenge him.

"Good Golly Miss Molly, she can sing and dance too," Layla muttered to her during a rousing rock'n'roll sing-along that saw Tammy break off from belting out the chorus to launch into an energetic jitterbug with one of the males. "We've got some stiff competition here."

"Yeah. It would be easier if she wasn't so

likable," Georgie whispered back. "Pity we couldn't have recruited her for *our* team."

Jerry saw them whispering, and came over. "Plotting, you two?" he asked cheerfully. Then, raising his voice, he said to the crowd at large, "Maybe we can convince Georgie to tell us what the future holds? What do you think? Will we ask her to get out that crystal ball?"

"*Jerry!*" Georgie glared at him. "Nobody wants to do that. We're having fun."

"Fortunes *are* fun," said a girl dressed in black and white, with a headscarf tied in a huge bow on top of her head. "C'mon, Georgie, do it! I didn't have time to see you for a reading today, and you're leaving tomorrow."

Layla tried to come to her rescue. "She's been telling fortunes all day. It's time to party."

"Yeah, there's too many of us," one of the others said, sounding regretful. "Would have been fun, though."

"I can't do it in public, anyway," Georgie said. "I need my crystal ball, and my trailer is way over next to the sales tent."

"I'll get your crystal ball," Jerry offered. "And you could use Tammy's trailer." He opened his arms wide, inviting everyone to support him. "What do you say, everyone? We can make it like speed dating. Names in a hat, six people, five minutes each. Half an hour, Georgie—just for fun?"

Like speed dating? Georgie thought, aghast. If Rosa were here, she'd have him for breakfast.

She looked around. Everyone was looking at her expectantly.

Dammit, Jerry! she thought for the one-millionth time in her life. She knew perfectly well what he was up to. With his sister tucked safely out of the way, he could talk his way into another sale or two.

"OK," she agreed, putting a good face on it. "But I'll go and get the crystal ball myself, thanks, Jerry." She didn't want him in her trailer when she was not there, but that was only part of it. The other thing was that the crystal ball was now *hers*. She didn't want Jerry's negative energy anywhere near it.

Half an hour, six fortunes. Who knew how *that* was going to turn out.

'Like speed dating', for heaven's sake.

CHAPTER 11

A Push from Rosa

The readings, Georgie had to admit, were fun. Especially in Tammy's lime-green-and-white vintage trailer. The girl had an eye for design.

Good choice by Jerry. *The jerk.*

The questions were predictable: everyone wanted to know about things like love, partners, travel, and career. To her relief—and surprise—even though she was limited to five minutes per person, her accuracy seemed to increase with each new client.

Practice makes perfect, she thought.

Her sixth and final reading was a woman in her early forties, who looked a lot younger with her Betty Bangs and smart navy sailor dress.

"Love your outfit," Georgie said admiringly.

"Thanks." The woman sat on the seat opposite Georgie and smoothed her skirt. "I'm Jenny." She opened her hands out in a "Whatever!" gesture. "Tell me anything you like."

"Just remember this is a 5-minute "speed fortune", according to Jerry," Georgie said for the sixth time that evening. "No guarantees!"

"So you say," Jenny said with a grin. "But your reputation has grown with each person who emerged from this trailer. Whatever you're doing, it's working."

Georgie said the first thing that came into her head. "Your partner doesn't really like your dress. But you wore it anyway. You're testing him…but you do love him." She took her hands off the crystal ball and glanced at it. The white mist in it was swirling almost angrily.

Anger? Did that mean Jenny was angry, or…?

Then she caught herself: analyzing things again. *Let go, Georgie.*

As soon as she relaxed, the words flowed.

"You have a lot of pent-up anger. Not with your current partner…someone else. Um, a previous love interest?" She closed her eyes for a moment, letting her mind sort through the information overload.

"Yes, that's it. You're not the only one to be fooled. He had several women."

Jenny's hands were clenched together in her lap. "Wow. Spot on. With everything."

Georgie sought something positive under the anger and found it. "You're thinking of getting married. To…Nathan? Nelson?"

"Nolan." Jenny nodded. "So, is that a good move?"

"I don't sense that you *shouldn't*," Georgie said cautiously. "I'm getting positive feelings about Nolan. What do you feel?"

"He's a nice guy," Jenny said. "Not perfect, which is good. I love him anyway. The last one was too perfect. Three other women he conned said the same thing. He was really good to them—before he fleeced them and left them." She picked at the white embroidered anchor on the full skirt of her dress. "Water under the bridge—but I'm still angry; as much at myself as anybody, for being so gullible."

Georgie sat back, her fingers still touching the crystal ball, and thought about how love and future happiness had been a recurring theme of her readings, even in one short week. "It's what we all want, isn't it? To be able to trust someone. To love without doubts." She had a sudden sense of a group of women, united. *Anger. Cleansing. Laughter.* "But you got your own back. You, and others…?"

"In a way," Jenny admitted. "We used social media to publish the details we had on him—but the police haven't caught him. That's what we want. Peter Fisher behind bars."

Another impression came through, very strongly. Georgie laughed. "You're going to get your wish. I see him in a cell. I don't know when, but that's where he'll end up."

Jenny sat forward, intrigued, staring at the crystal ball. "You can *see* him in there?"

"No, it's more of an impression… a message that comes in images. In the crystal ball, I usually just see a white mist—an occasional shadowy figure, if I'm lucky. It's more of a… *knowing.* But," she said with sudden confidence, "he's close to being caught."

"Can you see where he is?"

"No, sorry."

Then she felt the equivalent of a psychic shove; an almost physical thud in the middle of her back.

She gasped, straightened up, and asked silently: *Rosa? Is that you?*

Another push.

She *knew* that her great-grandmother was behind it.

"I feel that I'm supposed to ask you something else." At a loss, Georgie stared at Jenny. "Tell me anything you can. We'll see what shakes loose."

"Peter Fisher. Tall, dark hair, nice-looking, usually has his dog with him. Um… we've all got his picture on our Facebook pages, but the photo is from Ellie's old phone, and it's not a very good one. He was smart enough to avoid photos when he could. Last seen in Memphis."

Perhaps if she could see a likeness, something would register. Georgie dug her smartphone out of the deep pocket on her voluminous skirt and brought up the browser. She handed it to Jenny. "Can you show me the social media page you were talking about?"

"Sure." Intrigued, and looking hopeful, she tapped the screen a few times, then handed it back. "There. That's him."

Georgie stared at the photo. Jenny was right: it was terrible quality—blurred, as though he'd tried to turn away. It could almost have been anybody.

She scrolled down the page, skimming the women's stories.

Peter Fisher, conman. Preyed on women; won

their trust; gradually got more and more money out of them. Jenny had sold her car to give him money to invest, and bought an old rattler to get around in.

Georgie glanced up.

"I know," Jenny said wryly, her eyes on the screen. "I've kicked myself a thousand times. Stupid, huh?"

The sense that she was on to something got stronger.

Georgie moved on to the "Con Man Facts Box"—and froze.

Peter Fisher, alias Kenny Potts, alias Brian Marshall.

Brian Marshall… This time the feeling of being poked was so strong that she almost looked to see who was there.

"All *right*, Rosa," she said absently, her racing mind still making connections. "I get it."

"Who's Rosa?" Jenny asked.

"My interfering great-grandma. She owned the crystal ball before me," Georgie explained. She tapped the facts box on the screen. "He calls himself Kenny Potts and Brian Marshall too?"

"We think Brian Marshall is his real name. Well, at least, it's the only one that goes back to a real childhood—or so the PI we hired tells us. But he's probably not any of those now."

No, thought Georgie. Now, he's probably *Darryl* somebody.

She closed her phone and stood. "I think that's about it, Jenny. I'll let you know if I find out anything more."

"I hope you can." Jenny looked at her fiercely. "So we can all move on. I'd start my marriage happy if I knew he couldn't do this to anybody else."

Well, thought Georgie, he certainly won't be doing it to Kaylene.

CHAPTER 12

To the Rescue

Georgie's first instinct was to hitch up, jump in the car and drive to Dayton, but she didn't want to hitch up in the dark—and she had to pack up the sales tent anyway.

Why hadn't she got Kaylene's phone number?

Or Scott's, for that matter. She could have phoned him and asked him to make sure they didn't leave before she got there. Not that Scott could stand in the middle of the driveway and refuse to let them pass. Or could he? Georgie was prepared to do it, if that's what it took.

She was up at dawn to pack up, and by sunup was on the road, arrowing towards Dayton with the red light of dawn in her rearview mirror. Seventy-odd miles wasn't fair, considering the huge distances you could cover driving across the USA—but when you were in a hurry, it seemed to take forever.

When she finally pulled into the visitor's parking lot of the Dayton Happy Days RV Park, Georgie stuck her head out the window, peered down the access road, and breathed a sigh of relief. Kaylene's motorhome was still on the site. There was plenty of activity going on, though—both on her site and Darryl's next door.

Darryl aka Peter Fisher aka Kenny Potts aka Brian Marshall wasn't wasting any time.

She hoped she was right about all this.

"Georgie? What are you doing here?"

Startled, Georgie let out a tiny shriek of surprise. "Scott! Don't do things like that. You nearly gave me heart failure!"

"Yeah?" He raised an eyebrow and grinned. "Guilty conscience?" He followed the direction of her gaze. "Still worried about Kaylene, aren't you?"

She grabbed her smartphone and opened the browser, which was still set to Jenny's Facebook page. She scrolled down to the fuzzy photo of Brian-Kenny-Peter and handed it to him. "Here. Look. Does this look like Kaylene's Darryl?"

He squinted at it and then swiped to enlarge the image. "Could be. Difficult to tell. Yeah, kind of."

"Enlarging it doesn't help. I tried that. It's too low-res. Read the page."

Scott's good humor faded as he skimmed the content. "Real nice guy." He studied the picture again.

"I'm sure it's him. I know it sounds crazy, Scott, but I think Rosa was nudging me when I was doing the reading for one of the women last night. And this con-man, he went by "Brian" sometimes. It's the only connection I've been able to find."

He handed back the phone, and stood silently for a moment, watching Kaylene disappear into the motorhome with a folded camp chair.

"Scott?" *Please believe me,* she thought.

"I was thinking I could deactivate their codes so they can't get out," he said, looking at the boom gate, "but we have a few departures this morning. I'll have some unhappy people if I cause a traffic jam." He thought some more. "What I'll do is take the truck I use when I'm trimming back the trees and park it with the tail hanging over his site so he can't get out. I'll tell him I'll only be a moment if he tells me to move. That'll buy you some time."

"I've got to talk to Kaylene. Without him seeing me."

Scott glanced back at her gypsy trailer and grinned. "You think he hasn't seen you up here? You don't exactly fade into the background. Besides, you can't leave a trailer hitched up in the visitor's parking lot."

Georgie looked at him in astonishment. "You're going to impose the rules at a time like this?"

"No," he said, "I'm being devious. If you can see him, he can see us. You don't want him to run. I'll go down there and complain about people who think they're above the law and say I had to tell you to move to a temporary site. You can go down to 64. It's a pull-through." He pointed. "Next to the dumpsters."

"How do I talk to Kaylene without him seeing me?"

"Go to the office to sort out your site. To *pretend* to sort out your site. I'll make sure she goes there too."

Georgie thought about that for a moment. "He'll see us both go there. If he is this Brian Marshall, he must be getting nervous by now. I don't want him to get away. Did you see how much money he conned those women out of?"

"Okay." He ran a hand through his hair. "How's this: you take your trailer down to 64, and then head for the restrooms and go out of the door on the other side and up to the office—he won't be able to see you. Then I'll ask Kaylene to go and see reception because there's a problem with her credit card."

"It'll have to do." Conscious that time was passing, she made a decision. "Let's do it."

It all went as planned. Scott punched a code into the boom gate and watched her go by, and then reversed the RV Park truck out of its parking slot near the office and drove it down to the road near Darryl's site. In a show of what appeared to be negligent parking, he stopped and got out a pruning saw. Hopping out of her truck, Georgie saw him wave towards her trailer and make a laughing comment to Darryl.

Georgie hurried past them towards the restrooms.

Unfortunately, Kaylene came out of her RV just in time to see her walk by. "Georgie! What are you doing back here?"

Dammit. *Don't wreck this, Kaylene,* she thought. She looked back, waved, and then pointed at the restrooms, miming haste. "Sorry, Kaylene—I'm in a hurry! I'll catch up to say goodbye before you leave, okay?" She rushed on to the amenities block, barreled through, and was in the office within minutes.

A few minutes later, Kaylene came in and walked up to the counter. "Scott tells me there's a problem with my credit card. Kaylene Waters? Site 37?"

Georgie moved up beside her swiftly and touched her arm. "Can I speak with you for a moment, Kaylene?"

"What? Why?" No fool, Kaylene looked from the puzzled receptionist to Georgie and frowned. "What's going on?"

"Hear me out, Kaylene, please." Georgie took her through an open doorway into the adjoining mini-mart and brought up Jenny's Facebook page on her phone. "Look at this photo. Is it Darryl?"

Kaylene looked apprehensive. She took the phone and stared at the photo, then did the same as Scott, trying to enlarge it. "It looks like him." Then she peered closer and reduced the size of the picture again. Her face changed. "That's his cap. See the logo?"

The shape she pointed out looked like a white

blob, maybe a bird, to Georgie, but it obviously meant something to Kaylene.

"Read what it says on the page. Quickly."

As Kaylene skimmed through the text, the color drained from her face. "Peter Fisher…?"

"That means something to you?" Georgie's pulse quickened.

Kaylene looked up, her eyes bleak. "His phone rang one day while he was taking the dog for a walk. He'd been waiting for a callback from an insurance company so I thought I'd better answer it. It was a woman, demanding to speak to Peter. I told her she must have a wrong number, but she was insistent…and then Darryl came back and I handed it over to him." She swallowed hard. "He said it was just someone wanting his brother."

"*Does* he have a brother called Peter?"

"That's what he said on that day, but he and his family don't get on. He says he has good reasons for not wanting to contact them." Kaylene gave a ragged sigh. "I've done it again, haven't I? I just keep falling for losers. I was ready to sell up everything and move in with him." She shoved the phone back at Georgie. "And if I had, I'd be left with nothing. I'm a complete idiot."

"You're being a bit hard on yourself," said

Georgie sympathetically. "Our instinct is to trust people, don't you think? And Darryl is pretty plausible if he's conned other women too."

Kaylene stood there, staring into space. "Now what?"

"Now I think we'd better call the police. Sorry, Kaylene."

She closed her eyes, breathing shallowly. "Do what you have to."

One look at her told Georgie that there was no way Kaylene could pretend all was normal if she went back and talked to Darryl/Brian/Peter. "Can you just stay here? Out of the way? I'll tell Scott to keep him occupied."

Kaylene nodded, her lips tight.

Georgie made the call, and then went back the way she had come, out of the restrooms and back to her van. Scott saw her coming and just happened to be dumping branches in the truck when she walked past.

"All sorted?" he said cheerfully, winking.

"Yes, no thanks to you," Georgie said in a loud voice, sounding miffed. "I can move to Site 107 when the RV on it leaves. It's *miles* to walk to the restrooms. I'm not coming back here again." She stalked off and heard Scott say something to Darryl about women who were never pleased no matter what you did.

A backward glance showed an impatient Darryl pointing at his motorhome and then at his watch. She just hoped they had done enough to hold him until the police arrived.

CHAPTER 13

A Flash of Connection

Georgie had a ringside seat when the police turned up to talk to Brian Marshall. He didn't take kindly to their questions, hurling abuse at both the police and Kaylene—with a special tirade just for Georgie, when he spotted her in the background. The only effect that had was to convince the two officers that they should take him elsewhere for interrogation.

She felt bad for Kaylene, who said barely a word as she watched two cops take him away, and then just sat on the steps of her motorhome, staring into space, one arm around the neck of the dog Darryl/Brian had left behind.

As soon as the coast was clear, she went over to her.

"I'm so sorry, Kaylene." Georgie put her hand on Kaylene's shoulder. "You don't deserve any of this."

Kaylene said nothing for a moment and then sighed. "I don't think I do either. What is it about me that makes me a target for losers and criminals?"

"It won't always be this way." The words were meant to be comforting, but as Georgie spoke she had a strong sense that she was simply articulating a truth. This was a turning point for Kaylene.

"Are you just saying that, or do you… like, *know*?"

Georgie pushed aside the usual tendency to doubt herself. "I know."

"So I needed to have this happen?"

"You sensed something wasn't right, and you came to see me…and fate, or whatever, led me to Jenny, and we learned who Darryl was. Now he has finally been caught. You'll get justice, and so will the other women he's conned. That's a real step forward for you, Kaylene."

Kaylene said nothing for a moment and then sighed. "At least I didn't lose my home. It's too late for the others."

Georgie leaned down and hugged her. "True. Is there anything I can do, Kaylene?"

"No." Kaylene met her eyes and gave a tremulous smile. "Just thanks. I owe you a lot. I still can't believe you knew his name was Brian. I'll never poke fun at fortune-tellers again."

"You mean you *used to?*" asked Georgie in mock horror.

"Well, you know." Kaylene managed a small smile. "Fortune-tellers—you go to them for laughs, but you don't expect them to be real. If you know what I mean. Even though you might hope…"

Georgie knew what she meant all too well. Fortune-telling. It sounded like something you'd find in a sideshow.

She left Kaylene to think about what she'd do next, and went back to her trailer.

Her beautiful gypsy caravan.

Georgie stood back and stared at it, thinking. It had started out being just a pretty little home on wheels that she could take on the road to wage a sales war with her brother.

Georgie B. Goode, turning up in her cute vintage trailer, ready to draw vintage trailer fans like moths to a flame.

She'd done that, yes… but they weren't the only

people who had sought her out. Some people needed her other talents as well. The talents that Rosa had been nagging her about for years.

What was she going to do about that? Keep her crystal-ball-gazing as a party trick to help sell trailers… or take it seriously?

She knew what Rosa would say.

She knew what Jerry would say, too, but for different reasons from her great-grandmother. He didn't care about 'all that fortune-telling stuff'. He'd just tell her again to leave the selling to him and go play at being a gypsy psychic if that was what she wanted. Although he'd probably be miffed at losing his head designer. Even Jerry had to concede she was good at that.

She ran her finger over the carving on the outside of the Vardo trailer and thought about all those retro trailers that she'd so loved working on. She didn't want to give that up, either.

And she didn't want Jerry to win.

Why couldn't life be simple?

The sound of approaching footsteps brought her out of her reverie. Scott, she thought before she even turned around.

"Hey." He stopped a few feet away, watching

her curiously. "For someone who just apprehended a criminal, you don't look too happy."

"I didn't apprehend him, the police did. All I did was put two and two together. A lot of it was luck."

"Hmmm. No credit to the crystal ball, then?"

"Well, OK, some. And—" She cast him a side-long look. "And a bit of pushing from Rosa, I think. Somehow, she has a finger in this pie. You don't know how spooky she can be."

"I haven't met your great-grandma, but I've heard many people say the same thing about my mum. You'll always get the skeptics. Is that what's worrying you?"

"No. All this—it's just not me."

He didn't look convinced. "It's *part* of who you are. Only you can decide how big a part."

Georgie eyed him somewhat sourly. "You know, it would be so much easier if you just said 'Georgie, you should decorate and sell vintage trailers. Go and blast Jerry out of the water.'"

"You could do that too."

"You're no help at all."

"Not up to me." He smiled at her with true kindness. "There's no hurry. You'll know what's right, and *when* it's right." He nodded at her trailer. "Are you staying here tonight?"

"No, I'm heading on to Cleveland to meet up with Layla and some of the others from the vintage rally." Including Jenny, she thought, who would be delighted to hear of Brian Marshall's arrest. "We're going to visit the Rock and Roll Hall of Fame in Cleveland, and then in a couple of days we're moving on to Niagara Falls."

"Uh-huh." He offered her a hand. "I'd better get back to the office to tell them what's been going on down here. It's been nice meeting you, Georgie."

"You too." She took his hand, and almost snatched it back again when she felt the instant flash of connection. She sucked in a breath, staring at him.

Rosa was right. Somehow, this man was in her future.

Which meant his mother was also right.

Dammit. Did the whole world know what was going on in her life before she did?

His eyes glimmered with humor; almost as though he knew what she was thinking. Nice eyes, she thought. A warm, rich russet-brown color. The kind that sometimes went with red hair. Scott's hair wasn't red, though; it was a light ash brown with—

Belatedly realizing she was still holding his hand, she gave it a businesslike shake and dropped it like a hot potato.

"Well," she said with false cheer. "I'd better get going."

"Be seeing you."

He didn't say it with any loaded meaning, but she felt it anyway. Just as she felt his eyes on her while she swung herself into the cab of the truck and headed on up the road past him. When she looked into her side mirror, he was walking across to Kaylene, still sitting there cuddling the dog. She knew instinctively that he would offer what comfort he could.

Nice, she thought. He's a nice man.

Then she resolutely turned her thoughts to selling vintage trailers and seeing her sales soar past Jerry's.

Three weeks later, Georgie cruised slowly into the RV Expo behind her father and brother. The man himself, Johnny B. Goode, led the way, at the wheel of the Big Red Devil, as he had christened his Extreme RV. The crowds parted, awed, dying to look inside. The unveiling of Johnny's latest toy was a feature of every Expo.

His son Jerry B. Goode rolled along behind him, waving to the crowds from his seat high up in the cab of his black monster. It gleamed in the late morning sunshine, sending reflective flashes of light from the gold decals on the side.

And then came Georgie, a complete contrast in her gypsy trailer in shades of warm maroon and black with tasteful hints of gold. The Vardo trailer and truck with a matching canopy attracted as much attention as the two monster motorhomes that had preceded her. The crowds laughed and cheered, and she could hear cries of "Go, Georgie, go!" as she motored slowly by.

She had earned her place in this small convoy.

Because, she, Georgie B. Goode, had won. By a whisker. Or a wheel, if you like.

Jerry had done spectacularly well, coming in at 28 sales for the month.

Georgie—and her secret weapon, Layla—had gone one better. They had matched Jerry at 28 sales, thanks to not only sales on the road, but also to Georgie's phone calls and follow-ups to the list of clients that had been through the vintage trailer section in the past twelve months. That was Layla's idea.

And the nail in the coffin: Layla's new retro trailer, sale No. 29. The perfect vintage look, but with all the cunning modern twists that she and Georgie could think of.

Well, Georgie thought, if Jerry could include Tammy's new retro trailer, she could include Layla's.

Hah.

The vintage trailer section was *hers*.

CHAPTER 14

Good to Go

At nine o'clock that night, when the Expo gates had closed and the dinner with industry professionals was over, Georgie joined her family for the traditional celebratory drink at the end of Day 1. As always, the venue was Johnny B. Goode's latest and most extreme RV.

You could hold a wedding in this thing, Georgie thought, looking around her as she settled into the sumptuous white leather lounge. All four slide-outs were extended, and it was more like an apartment than an RV. The only thing missing was a rooftop garden, and she was expecting her father to figure out that one Real Soon Now.

She watched him while he popped the cork of a

bottle of Dom Pérignon and busied himself filling glasses with bubbles, talking the whole time.

"…best show ever! We've already got more than a dozen orders for this baby. They've never seen anything like it. We've hit one out of the park this time." With a wink, he handed one glass to Angela and another to Tammy, who seemed to have become part of the family very quickly. Tonight, she had abandoned her rockabilly persona in favor of an elegant 30s style dress and Rita Hayworth hair. Perched next to Jerry on the two-seater opposite, she still looked retro, but also like the perfect accessory for his big black and gold motorhome.

She had been a real find, Georgie admitted, not only for Jerry but also for the Johnny B. Goode RV Empire.

Her father passed a flute to Jerry, and another to Georgie. "This is the perfect drop to celebrate. Limited edition, so sip it slowly!" He patted her on the shoulder and leaned down to whisper, "Great job, girl. I'm proud of you."

"Thanks." Georgie avoided Jerry's eye. He was putting a good face on it for the evening, but she knew he'd still be smarting. Jerry didn't like to lose.

"And one for my grandmother, who inspired all this—the original nomadic soul." Johnny handed a glass that was more froth than bubbles to Rosa, sitting quietly beside Georgie, and then moved to stand next to his wife before raising his glass. "To the Johnny B. Goode RV Empire and all who work there. This year has been real 'good' to us!"

They all laughed dutifully at the inevitable 'good' joke and raised their glasses in turn. "To Johnny B. Goode!" they chorused.

"Well." He cast a look around, his smile growing even wider, if that were possible. "This year was a landmark year. Not only have sales increased by seventeen percent overall, but our vintage trailer division has also really taken off—both restorations for selected clients, and the modern trailers with a customized retro look. Gypsy trailers—who would have thought?" He nodded at Georgie and then moved his gaze to Jerry. "The competition between my two great kids added a new dimension this year. You both did a terrific job, but the winner—by one sale—is Georgie. Who now heads up the vintage trailer division." He raised his glass again. "To Georgie."

"To Georgie!" the others echoed. Even Jerry managed a wry grin and a tilt of his glass in her direction, but beside her, Rosa snorted.

"Thanks, Dad. And thank you all for your good

wishes. But—" She paused for effect, and then looked straight at Jerry. "I've changed my mind."

That floored them. Her father's jaw dropped. Jerry stared at her, his smile fading. Tammy looked puzzled, sending a quick glance from her to Jerry and back again.

"Jerry can have the job," she went on. "He's right, he's good at sales. I'm OK, but I don't love it. What I do love is being on the road, meeting people who live the lifestyle. I'd rather lead the road team."

"You've got to be kidding," Jerry said. "Live on the *road*?"

"Well, yes," Georgie said. "Like a lot of our clients."

"In a *gypsy trailer*?" His voice edged a note higher.

"Why not? Rosa did it for years," Georgie pointed out. "And she didn't have portable solar panels and inverters and an Internet connection."

Rosa snorted again.

"I think it's brilliant," Tammy said, leaning forward, her blue eyes sparkling. "People love meeting Georgie when they travel. And she's such a good fortune-teller! Do you know what she did? She—"

Knowing that Tammy had heard on the 'nomad grapevine' about exactly how she had found the answer to the Brian Marshall con man puzzle, Georgie hastily cut her off. She didn't need to give Rosa any more fuel for the fire. "I won't necessarily be telling any fortunes, Tammy, but I want to travel. It's the ideal solution. I'll lead the vintage trailer road team, and I get to have fun."

"But you're the head designer," Jerry objected. "You can't disappear for months at a time."

"Hire another one. There are plenty out there."

"You'll still consult on design, won't you?" Tammy said, her forehead creasing. "You've put your stamp on things."

"Tammy, you have an excellent eye," Georgie pointed out, remembering how comfortable she'd felt reading fortunes in Tammy's lime green and white trailer. "Just look at your vintage trailer. People loved it—and it was all your work."

Tammy sat back, looking thoughtful. "That's true."

With that, the worst was over. Even her father—who liked to be in control as much as Jerry—came around to thinking it could be a very good thing to have his daughter out there on the road.

Finally, Rosa stirred. She had said nothing—apart uttering a few snorts and haughty sniffs—as the discussion was going on, but now Georgie sensed that she wanted to have her say.

She had been expecting it.

"Help me up, girl. They make these modern sofas much too low," she grumbled, putting a hand on Georgie's elbow. "Takes half an hour to struggle out of one."

Obediently, Georgie stood and helped Rosa to her feet.

"Come with me," she ordered. "I want to talk to you in private." Ignoring the others, she led Georgie into the bedroom and shut the door firmly behind them.

"Get out the crystal ball," she said, sitting on the bed.

Georgie didn't bother asking how Rosa knew that she'd put it in her father's safe for the duration of the Expo. Rosa knew everything. Kneeling, she opened a small cupboard door and tapped in the combination of the safe behind it.

The crystal ball, still wrapped in its black cloth, hummed in her hands. Did it want to go back to Rosa? Maybe Rosa intended to resume ownership since Georgie had disappointed her by continuing to work in sales. Georgie felt a brief flash of rebellion. She didn't want to give up the ball; she was just beginning to know it.

"Come sit beside me." Rosa patted the mattress.

Georgie sat and reluctantly held out the crystal ball to her great-grandmother.

"No," Rosa said. "I told you, it's yours now. You're the next in line."

"So you keep saying. What if I don't want to?"

Rosa cackled, her dark eyes snapping with amusement. "You can't fool me, girl. You've felt the call. Even if you did need a good push now and then."

"It *was* you." Georgie felt a strange mixture of relief and annoyance. "I wasn't imagining it when I was doing the reading for Jenny. And—" she stopped, eyeing the old woman. She had been going to say: "—and you were there when I was reading for Scott," but that was more…private.

Rosa didn't do private. "And your Leo, too, yes."

"I can't do readings with you looking over my shoulder like that."

"Once you open up to it fully, I won't have to."

Which probably meant that, for a while, she

could expect to have Rosa butting in whenever a reading didn't go the way it was supposed to. It would be like having an irascible genie living with you. Except she couldn't stash Rosa in a lamp and seal her in with a cork.

"I just want to enjoy life on the road and boost sales in the vintage trailer division," she said. "You heard me out there. I'm not a real gypsy fortune-teller, like you."

The look Rosa gave her was half exasperated and half superior. "Look into the crystal ball. See what it tells you."

For a moment Georgie contemplated refusal, but the crystal ball in her hands hummed again and it seemed to be beyond her power to resist. Slowly, she unwrapped it and laid the black velvet cloth on the bed.

The mist inside the crystal swirled and leaped.

Georgie felt herself grow warm, and some part of her went to meet the knowledge that lay within that mist.

She had to go to California.

Her forehead creased, and she fought it.

NO. She had been planning to head south, not west.

Los Angeles. Something was waiting for her

in L.A.

Inside her, something shifted, and, coming from somewhere else, Georgie felt a wave of grief and the need. She closed her eyes and slumped.

Dammit.

"You see?" said Rosa. This time her voice was quiet, almost hypnotic. "You feel the call. You must go; there is no choice." Her gnarled old hand reached out and touched Georgie. Strangely, her touch was reassuring. "Stop fighting it, girl."

"Is this what it was like for you? Did you have to just travel around, letting the crystal ball decide where to go?"

Rosa laughed, her harsh cackle back again. "Good heavens, no. *Sometimes* it called me. The rest of the time, I went where I fancied—or where the family wanted to go. Life isn't all about duty, girl."

When Georgie looked up, she was startled to see her great-grandmother wink.

"Your Leo is out there, too. Hadn't you better go find him?"

Dammit.

Interfering great-grandmas…

"Well, girl. Are you good to go?"

Georgie gave up. "All *right*, Rosa. You win. I'm good to go."

Dear Reader,

About eighteen months before I started writing about Georgie, two things happened that eventually came together and resulted in this book…and the rest of the Gypsy Trailer Cozy Mystery Series.

The first thing: I was traveling with my husband in our own RV and we stopped at an RV park in a small country town. It happened to be the day after a festival, and one of the first things we saw was a fantastic old gypsy caravan. I discovered later that it was called a Bowtop, and it had been rescued from obscurity and pressed into service by a gypsy fortune-teller. She took it to various markets and towns, and set up a tent nearby to tell fortunes; she used the caravan for sleeping.

I took photos, thought how great it was, and moved on to explore the rest of the country.

Fast forward a year or so, and we were in an entirely different part of the country—and this time, we found ourselves in an RV park surrounded by gorgeous vintage setups. I was completely won over. I took photo after photo, and chatted to lively women dressed in retro fashions and cats-eye sunglasses, visited rockabilly events, and enjoyed afternoon tea eaten from delicate plates with floral retro patterns. I realized that this was a whole life-style for some people: vintage trailers, vintage cars, and vintage clothes.

A few months after that, I decided I'd write a mystery series—a cozy mystery series, which would actually be more cozy puzzles, because I didn't really want to have a corpse in each story. Hmm, I thought, who could the sleuth be? Where could I have these stories take place?

In a variety of locations, I thought. Someone could be traveling around, as I like to do, and find a mystery—or puzzle—in each place. That's when everything suddenly came together. Travel, vintage and retro trailers, and a gypsy fortune-teller who finds herself solving mysteries!

So here you are, now at the end of the second book in the series!

Here's an invitation for you: subscribe to my newsletter to get news of new releases, bonus books, specials and a sneak peek at scenes from my books in progress. As a welcome gift, you'll also receive a copy of *Fortune's Wheel*, the prequel to the Georgie series.

Here's your chance to find out more about the

intriguing old woman that Georgie sees as a kind of taciturn genie. Whether she wanted to believe it or not, from birth Georgie was destined to follow in Great-Grandma Rosa's footsteps—as well as inherit her crystal ball!

If you haven't already done so, visit my website below to join other readers and download your copy.

MargMcAlister.com/free-georgie-book/

ABOUT THE AUTHOR

Marg McAlister is the author of the popular Georgie B. Goode Cozy Mystery series (set in the USA) and Series 2 (Australian RV Adventure series), also featuring Georgie.

Marg lives by the sea on the mid-north coast of NSW, but she and her husband spend part of the year on The Gemfields in Central Queensland, living off the grid on their mining claim. While her husband digs for sapphires and zircons, operates the wash plant and drives around dirt tracks, Marg is usually writing—or socializing!

Marg is also the author of a series of books for aspiring writers, and the owner of Blue Gem Publishing, which publishes books in a range of genres.

Next in This Series:
GEORGIE BE GOOD

Chapter 1

Fortune-telling had its moments.

The woman sitting opposite Georgie frowned, cast a dissatisfied look around the trailer, and pursed her lips. Her eyes darted from the candle flickering on the carved shelf to the stained glass windows and then to the soft drapes around the bed before they returned to the Georgie herself. Her eyes narrowed. Every inch of her said: *You're a charlatan and your gypsy trailer's a fake.*

She heaved herself up off the small bench seat tucked in behind Georgie's compact kitchen table. "Well, I guess my time's up. I have to tell you, though; I don't feel that I've got my money's worth. I haven't learned anything new."

Her pronouncement didn't surprise Georgie one little bit. The moment Marcie Kruger had heaved her bulk through the door twenty minutes earlier, wearing a look of permanent petulance, she had known that this wasn't going to go well. That had been confirmed when Georgie rested her fingers on her great-grandmother's crystal ball and picked up on a massive disagreement looming between Marcy and her family; an estrangement that would last for years. She had attempted to touch on the issue delicately by suggesting that diplomacy might be in order when interacting with her children, but that idea had been shot down in flames.

"I'm not pandering to that lot," Marcie said with a ferocious frown. "All out for what they can get, always have been. I was delighted when they finally all left home." She frowned at the crystal ball. "Are you sure you didn't get anything about who I should live with?"

What she was really asking was which ancient relative would die quickly and leave her the most money in return for some grudging home care, and that particular information hadn't been revealed to Georgie. Which was good, because she felt no inclination to help Marcie Kruger at all.

"Sorry," she said, smiling pleasantly. "Nothing at all. But you know this is principally for entertainment, right?"

"Huh. That's what you all say, but some of my friends have been to fortune-tellers who know their stuff. I'll have to ask who they went to." She wrenched the door open and lumbered down the steps, proclaiming loudly to anyone who cared to listen, "Waste of time, waste of money!"

Georgie sighed and looked at the antique clock on the wall. Marcie had been the only customer this morning, thank God. Sooner or later, the unknown person who had drawn her toward L.A. would turn up, but it didn't look like it would be today.

She could go and find Layla and relax for a while; enjoy the balmy Santa Monica weather while they watched the crowds wander around the weekend market.

Even as the thought came into her mind, her phone rang. She glanced at the display and raised her eyes heavenward. It was her scheming, conniving, smooth-talking-salesman brother, Jerry.

Could the day get any worse?

"Georgie! How are you?" Jerry's voice was filled with manufactured excitement, which put her on guard immediately. "I've got some great news, kiddo. We're moving the vintage and retro division to its own premises!"

Georgie scowled at the phone. *You're an idiot,*

Georgie, she told herself. The minute she'd agreed to let him handle vintage and retro she should have known how things would go.

"What do you mean, to its own premises? What are you up to, Jerry?"

"Georgie." He managed to sound hurt and patronizing at the same time. "Give me some credit. You've been doing so well with sales that we thought it deserved to be a specialist unit. Anyone who wants one of our vintage trailers can go directly there. The reno team will be based there too. It's perfect."

Georgie moved the phone away from her ear and glared at his photo on the screen. "Vintage was perfect right where it was. You know we were able to pick up sales from people who were there to look at other RVs. Why move? And where to?"

"Not far away."

"Where?"

"Pineberry Street."

"I've never heard of it. Where's Pineberry Street?"

"Out near Vic's repairs."

Vic's? It took her a moment to remember who Vic was, and then a picture of a scruffy, rat-like little man came to mind. He looked like a tramp, but Jerry and her father loved him because he could work magic with engines. Aghast, she conjured up a picture of Vic's run-down neighborhood.

"Out *there*? You have got to be kidding." Then the light dawned. "You're going to use one of those properties that Dad bought last year. The ones he was planning to *demolish*."

"Think long-term, Georgie-Porgie. It will be prime real estate when the market recovers."

Georgie squeezed her eyes shut tight and recalled the tired streets with boarded-up businesses and overgrown lots. They couldn't do this to her vintage and retro division. She wouldn't allow it. "Not a chance, Jerry. I'll fight you on this."

"You'll be fighting Dad too, then," he said smoothly. "He needs the space for his VIP suite and Platinum Customer Care program."

Dammit, she thought. If that was the case, she'd lost. Her father had been talking about this forever: something else to make the Johnny B. Goode RV Empire the only place to buy your RV. Luxurious guest rooms, a weeklong stay for premium customers, advanced driver training, and complimentary coupons for five-star RV parks.

"Of course Dad plans to give the Pineberry

Street place a facelift," Jerry said, as though handing out a sweet to a fractious toddler.

"And does he plan to smarten up everything within six streets as well?" asked Georgie crossly. One of these days she was going to do something horrible to Jerry. "This wasn't part of the agreement when I agreed to let you manage the division."

"Managing the division means doing the best thing for the whole RV Empire as well as vintage. It's a done deal. I'm just doing you the courtesy of letting you know. C'mon, Georgie, be good now."

Aaargh. If there was one thing she was heartily sick of hearing, after nearly thirty years of it, it was that tired old 'Georgie, be good' line. She'd heard every possible play on words associated with her family name.

Feeling steam coming out of her ears, she swiped at the red 'end call' button and sat there, fulminating. They couldn't relegate her vintage trailers to a broken-up ex-parking lot. Pulling up a few weeds and slapping a bit of paint on those decrepit buildings wouldn't be enough.

The sneaky rat. This so wasn't going to happen.

She would go and find Layla, the other member

of her on-road sales team, and see what she thought.

On hearing about Jerry's perfidy, Layla poured steaming tea from a buttercup-yellow teapot into baby-pink cups, pointed a finger at Georgie, and said: "Phone Tammy."

The teapot and cups picked up the delicate sorbet colors of Layla's retro trailer. Sitting in it was like entering a simpler and happier world. Layla herself looked like a smart 50s housewife, decked out in comfortable scarlet capris and a raspberry red checked shirt with the tails tied at her waist. Her hair was tied up in a matching headscarf. She even had lipstick on.

"How can you look this put-together this early in the morning?" Georgie muttered, picking up the teacup and glancing down at her hastily donned dark gypsy skirt and blouse. She felt dowdy in comparison.

"Dress-up," Layla said. "I love it. And it helps to sell retro trailers. It's the whole look that gets people in."

Georgie smiled despite herself, and then

returned to the subject. "I can't phone Tammy. She's Jerry's girlfriend, she'll be on his side."

"Wanna bet?" Layla said. "When have you ever seen Tammy dress in anything but vintage?"

Never, Georgie had to admit. "But she's sleeping with the enemy. She's back in Elkhart with Jerry more than she's out with the road team now."

"True. But she's one of us at heart. She loves retro. She's not going to want to see it relegated to some seedy area six miles away." She nodded at the phone next to Georgie's elbow. "Phone her."

With a sigh, Georgie did.

The phone rang several times, and then Tammy picked up. "Hang on a minute," she said immediately, and then Georgie heard her say "It's my aunt. I'll take it outside."

Georgie covered the phone and whispered to Layla, "Something's up!" and angled the phone so she could hear too.

After a few moments, Tammy came on again. "Georgie?"

"You were there when he phoned me just then, weren't you?" Georgie said.

"Yes. I'm so sorry, Georgie. I don't know how he could do this to us!" Tammy's voice was low and very cross. "We've got to come up with a plan. This can't happen."

Layla mouthed, *I told you so*, and sat back with a satisfied look.

Georgie's heart lightened. "Tammy, I always said I wouldn't wish this on my worst enemy… but will you please marry my brother? I need an ally."

"Oh, he's not that bad." Tammy's voice softened. "I know he's a schemer, but he makes me laugh."

"That's what my mother said about my father," Georgie said, "until she couldn't stand it anymore and they divorced."

"Hmm. Yes, but I think I've got his measure. Give me some time to mull over this, and I'll call you back. We've got a customer with us right now."

"Great." Georgie relaxed, feeling marginally better. Although he tried to hide it, she did think Jerry was besotted with Tammy. If anyone could change his mind, she could. "Call tonight. Layla and I are busy all day."

"Ask her what she's wearing," Layla said.

"I heard that." Tammy laughed. "Vintage 1950s organza hand-painted dress. Cost a fortune, but I couldn't resist." Her voice dropped. "Jerry loves it. Drives him crazy."

"Oh please," Georgie said. "Too much information."

"Think of it as a weapon," Tammy said. "He'll be putty in my hands. Gotta go."

Layla sat back and popped a piece of toast into her mouth. "I always did like Tammy," she said with a grin.

Find it at your preferred bookstore or online:
https://books2read.com/Georgie-Be-Good

www.ingramcontent.com/pod-product-compliance
Lightning Source LLC
Chambersburg PA
CBHW031418200726
48285CB00017BA/2434